Rob Slattery lives in Dublin with his wife and three children.
Two Watches is his first novel.

For Mum, Dad and Bee. Missed and remembered every day.

Rob Slattery

TWO WATCHES

AUSTIN MACAULEY PUBLISHERS™

LONDON • CAMBRIDGE • NEW YORK • SHARJAH

A CIP catalogue record for this title is available from the British Library.

ISBN 9781398460812 (Paperback)
ISBN 9781398460829 (ePub e-book)

www.austinmacauley.com

First Published 2022
Austin Macauley Publishers Ltd®
1 Canada Square
Canary Wharf
London
E14 5AA

Thanks to Jenny, Lucy, Adam and Phoebe for all the fun.

And thanks to Gem and Rach – the WhatsApp group has lifted my spirits and made me laugh through sad times!

I always wanted Dad to write a book. He didn't, so I had to do it for him.

A man who has not prepared his children for his own death has failed as a father. Have I ever failed you?

King T'Chaka, Black Panther, 2018.

Chapter 1

Dublin, July 2020.

My father died last week.

Even as I read that line aloud, I cannot believe it is true. My dad. Gone.

Death is quite an incredible thing. It happens everywhere, every second of every day and yet when it happens to you, it feels like you are the only person suffering, the only one who will ever feel such grief. One day you wake up and all is well in the world. By the end of the day, you are trying to get to grips with the fact you will never get to see someone again. Or talk to them. Hear their voice. Ever again. I think that is the part I am finding most difficult to comprehend. It makes you realise that we really do need to seize each day in life. Enjoy every day. Treasure people. Tell them how you feel – once they are gone, you cannot.

I refresh the condolences page on rip.ie about twenty times a day. It is a website that announces deaths in Ireland. People can not only find out the funeral arrangements there but also leave messages of condolence. There have only been two updates in the last 3 days. That page was an incredible surprise. For the first few days after his post went up, there were messages appearing every couple of minutes. Comments and stories that old friends and colleagues had left, finding out little pieces of new information about his life. But no more. The text messages and Mass cards have stopped arriving too. I remember that from when my Mum died – I loved opening them. People are so thoughtful and caring around death. But when they stop coming, it hurts even more. Because life has moved on.

I am desperately trying to remember everything. I have a notebook I carry with me all the time – I am writing it all down. I find writing cathartic. But I am also so scared I will forget some part of his life.

I did not talk to him every day. He rarely rang me – "you're probably too busy" he would say when I would ask him why not. It was not some sort of bullshit, always-rosy relationship. It was real. And I miss him. I miss knowing that he is there – even if I do not talk to him or see him all the time.

When I think back to my childhood, I automatically think of my mum. I spent a lot of time in her company – I was the archetypal 'Mummy's Boy'. When my mum died, I honestly thought I would never recover. I felt like my heart had literally been ripped out of my chest. My dad got me through it. Not necessarily, in the way, he acted or cared for me, but more so that I knew I had to be strong for him. His loss was more than mine was. She was his wife. His life. In trying to look after him and making sure that he was ok, it stopped me from dwelling on the grief I felt. Sounds odd but I think it helped.

My dad and I had a different relationship. It was not the same as the bond I had with Mum. Maybe it is the same with all fathers and sons. Or Mothers and sons for that matter. I worshipped my dad when I was younger. I wanted to be him.

And when I look around at my friends who are fathers of sons now and indeed look at my own son, I see that this is true of nearly every boy. Your dad is your hero. Then, as you grow up and get older, this changes. You see flaws. You realise that they cannot actually save the world or that they do not actually know everything. Dad and I began to fight and bicker with each other, as I grew up. Nothing ever serious but I always felt my mum had my side.

For a lot of my younger life, Dad was away with work. I never really knew where if I am honest. I am not sure I even asked that much. I know at one point he was away for 6 months and was scared that I would not recognise him when he returned. I did.

I do have some vivid memories from my childhood that stand out. When I was little and dad would put me to bed, as he was leaving my room he would always say, "I love you."

And I would always reply, "I love you more".

Dad would pause, smile, say "Impossible", and then turn off the light.

I loved the story about the day I was born. Two workers were roofing our garage when the news came through and dad in his excitement at hearing the news called them inside and shared a full bottle of whiskey with them toasting my arrival. I do not know if this story is true – in fact, I do not even know if I was told it that way. But it is the one I like to remember.

I remember clearly following him around the garden as he mowed the lawn. I had a toy wooden trolley that I would pretend was cutting the grass and follow in his footsteps. We lived in the countryside and the lawn felt enormous to me. I would spend hours faithfully following him around the garden. Kicking a football and passing a rugby ball with Dad and my big brother Tom. For hours on end. Talking about everything and nothing and sometimes not even talking at all. In my head, I was playing at Old Trafford or Lansdowne Road.

Sport had always been our thing. Dad was from Kilkenny, so hurling was in his blood. However, he loved all sports. That love and passion were passed on to both my brother and me. We played everything we could when we were younger. Winters were filled with soccer, rugby and GAA; summers spent re-enacting Wimbledon or chasing runs at Lords. And sport has played a huge part in my life. When I look back, moments in my life always seem to be linked to some big sporting event, as a reference point for my memory.

Dad took me to Old Trafford to see Manchester United play Aston Villa in December 1993. I was 13. It was just the two of us. I was so excited I could not sleep the night before. The excitement of catching the plane with other supporters, the anticipation building. Before kickoff, we went to the Manchester United superstore and Dad bought me an Eric Cantona T-shirt. I still have that T-shirt – I found it the other day when I was clearing out the attic. I can remember entering the stadium, in awe of its size and I remember vividly walking out to our seat with Tina Turners 'Simply the Best' blaring out of the speakers. United won 3-1 that day. Cantona scored twice but Andrei Kanchelskis was the star. The noise of the crowd every time he got the ball and set off down the wing. Pure, raw speed. Dad cheering and roaring – immersed in the whole experience just as much, or in fact, even more than I was. Our excitement of seeing Roy Keane and Denis Irwin, the Irish lads, in the flesh. On the way back to the Airport, Dad nearly fell out of a lift. It was one of those ones where you enter on one side but exit on the other. He was leaning against the doors when they opened. We laughed for a good hour about it. United were our team.

In 1996, I spent a term of school at a boarding school in France. Every week I received a package from Dad– clippings from the sport pages of the newspapers filling me in on Manchester United and the epic 1995/96 season. Remember this was before social media or even mobile phones. A bit of context – it had been an incredible season. During pre-season, Manchester United had sold Paul Ince, Mark Hughes and Kanchelskis – and not replaced them with any new signings. Alex Ferguson, their legendary manager, was convinced that the new academy players coming through could fill their boots. Beaten 3-1 at Aston Villa in their first game, Alan Hansen made his famous "you can't win anything with kids" statement on the BBC. This was the Manchester United of Beckham, Scholes, Nicky Butt, and the Neville Brothers. With Roy Keane adding the bite. But also of Eric Cantona. 'Il Dieu'. Eric was my hero and Dad's favourite. This season was his return from his ban for famously Kung Fu kicking a fan at an away match at Crystal Palace. Typical Cantona. That had happened in January 1995, and I can remember being in the car with Dad on the way to school and hearing all about it on the radio. We could not believe it. He had jumped into the crowd and kicked a supporter! Dad clearly did not want me to think this was acceptable behaviour but had a glint in his eye and a sly smile, telling me how bad it was. Cantona served his suspension and returned in October and played such a pivotal role in United winning the championship. United were 12 points behind Newcastle with just 15 games to go in the season. However, in an incredible run of matches in March and April, starting with a 1-0 win against Newcastle, Cantona scored in six games in a row. Five of these were the only goal of the game including four, 1-0 victories. I left for France in April and so would wait longingly for my package to arrive every week. I would rip the package open and dive straight into the match reports. From The Irish Times, The Independent and The Sunday Times. I relived all of these wins, watching from afar, as United edged closer. Dad would also include a note – nothing long but just filling me in on the lines he thought were the best or maybe a small description of a goal he saw. And always a reference to Cantona – how he was guiding the kids to victory.

Manchester United sealed the league title with a 3-0 win away at Middlesbrough. They also reached the FA Cup final that year. And they were playing Liverpool. In the lead-upto the game, Dad again posted me bags stuffed with all of the build-up from the newspapers. On the day of the match itself, he arranged to call me at the school after full time to let me know the result. I can still remember the call – he pretended they had lost but then roared down the phone that they had won 1-0. Not only that but Cantona had scored the winner. He was exuberant, describing in detail how the ball had dropped to Eric at the edge of the box, and he had volleyed it through a crowd of players with just 4 minutes left. I felt like I was there beside him. Hanging up the call, I made my way back to the dormitories where my new classmates were waiting. They all knew about the match and played up the French connection with Eric. A huge cheer went up as I pumped my fist, grinning from ear to ear. I felt 10 feet tall. It was as if I had won the FA Cup myself.

Since that season, I have often thought about how much excitement I would have as the post arrived for me that term. Going to matches, watching them live on TV or checking apps on my phone – they do not create the same feeling as I had as I would rip open the packages to devour the lines of text. Sports writing was a thing of beauty back then. Con Houlihan, James Lawton, and Hugh McIlvanney – legends of their profession. All gone now. Those feelings, not only given to me by the writing but also given to me by my dad and his love of writing and his excitement to share it with me, are irreplaceable. That feeling we were sharing something special. Something only he and I could talk about properly. Our thing.

At home, Dad did not have the attention span to watch a full match. He would get so excited about big games – particularly hurling games – but it was the anticipation and build-up he enjoyed nearly more than the match itself. He loved reading the sportswriters and talking about what might happen. Most of the time, when the match actually started, he would get up and go for a walk. It used to infuriate me – particularly in later life when I would call into him especially to watch a match with him. And he would be gone – off around the garden, unable to watch the whole thing. He would come back, normally with about 20 minutes to go, asking all sorts of irritating questions about who scored and how.

He also played golf all his adult life and instilled a love of the game in me. We played a lot of golf together. And golf is a great game for relationships. After all, you spend 4-5 hours at a time in each other's company. There were many times that we would be having an argument at home and barely speaking to each other. Yet would still head off to the golf course to play 18 holes. By the time we returned, the argument would be long forgotten, replaced with tales of birdies or brutal drives and missed putts. Recently we talked about his last ever game of golf and how he could not recall it. How much he missed it. Even just getting out for a couple of holes as he got older. Golf is a game with enjoyment for everyone who plays. Hearing him talk of a par that he made on Stroke Index 1 and in the same breath, giving out about how he could hardly walk anymore, confirms this. I made sure I took Dad's golf clubs from his apartment. He had kept hold of them and his golf shoes. I suppose he thought he might make a comeback. I could not see them being thrown away.

Watching golf also brought him great joy. He liked the fact he could turn it on and have it in the background, safe in the knowledge that it would be on for hours. If I think back over the last 10 years, the majority of the phone calls I can remember I made to Dad were about golf. And most of them were about Padraig Harrington and Shane Lowry and their respective performances. Watching Shane Lowry win The Open with Dad at my side is a memory I will never forget. I do not know who I was happier for – Shane or Dad. If I close my eyes, I can see him now, arms raised with a beer in his hand, eyes looking like he crying, because he was, and cheering loudly. Happy times.

I do wonder what sporting occasions will feel like now without him here to talk to about them. What if Shane had not won The Open then, but instead won it next year. Or the Irish rugby team win the Grand Slam. Will it be the same? The answer is No, it will not.

Chapter 2

I have this awful feeling that the rest of the world is moving on. Life goes on. People go back to work. News headlines change. I want to slow time down. I want to remember all of this. I do not want to forget. Anything. I do not want to stop crying at random moments. I feel that if I do, I will have moved on too. And he deserves more.

I would knock on his door, and I would hear a shout of something indiscernible from inside. And the sound of shuffling. And humming. Not a song I could identify – just humming. And then the door would open. And a smile. Or maybe not. A little list of jobs he would have for me was written on the back of his New Yorker calendar. And he would have kept several days of the calendar to show me – he found them funny or thought I would like them. He would sit in his chair. I would move a chair opposite. And we would chat – just catching up. Not talking about anything in particular.

Now, when I walk past his window by the river and lookup – it will not be him I see. Or his things. His tablecloth. His lamp. His bench facing the sun. His pots of flowers. All gone. I would sometimes walk by, and he would be sitting in the sunshine, cap on, I could see the sun cream on his face not rubbed in. He would be deep in a book. Miles away. I would not disturb him every time. Sometimes I would simply look up at him. Wondering where he was in his head and what he was thinking about. Eventually, I would find that a bit odd so I would call up. And he would nearly jump off the balcony in fright. So easily startled. Then he would see me, and a smile would break over his face. "Ah Will! Are you coming up?" Always his response no matter what the time of day. When Matthew, my son, was small and would wake brutally early in the summer mornings, I would creep out of the house early with him, trying not to wake my wife and bring him for a walk. We would head for the river and past Dad's and there would be no sign of him. I would ring him, later on, to tell him we were there.

"I was up!" he would cry. "You must've just missed me."

It became like a competition – he loved being awake early. Listening to the news. Finding out what happened the previous night, as he was rarely awake past 9:30 p.m. And a nice cup of tea. He would potter into his kitchen, make it, and bring it back to bed. Then perhaps, a bit of Lyric FM to get the day started. Then up and make his beloved porridge. God, that man loved a bowl of porridge. You have to soak it the night before you know.

His phone number is still on my recent calls screen on my mobile phone. With every day and every new call, it moves closer to disappearing. And I really do not want it to. But time goes on. And life moves on.

I miss ringing him when I hear a bit of news on the radio he would like. It would not have been a long conversation, but it would have been fun. Or Shane missing the cut in his first tournament back post the COVID break.

I will miss him, and I will always miss him. But I am so glad that we got to spend so much time together over the last 10 years.

As more time passes and days turn into weeks, more memories come flooding back. Some small, some big. Things happen around me – things I would like to talk to him about. Other people die – famous people. Jack Charlton died earlier this year. Jack was 85. The thing about Jack dying and the reason why it triggered such an outpouring of emotion and grief from all of us was not so much about the man himself passing away. He was a good age. No, it was about the memories that his passing reminded us all of. The memories of the people you spent that amazing time with. The memories of how we all felt during a glorious period in the country. I do not remember Euro 88. However, I remember Italia 90. And the pure excitement. Packie Bonners save from Daniel Timofte. I am not sure anyone in Ireland will ever forget poor Daniel's name. Folklore.

Then USA 94. The excitement of getting an Ireland World Cup T-shirt. Dad brought me to an event in town to watch a screening of Ireland – Italy. I think he had nabbed the tickets through work. I can remember the excitement I felt getting ready to go into town – not only for the match itself but also because I going out to watch it with my dad. All of my friends were watching it at home. And then we won! Ray Houghton. 1-0. A wonder goal. Paul McGrath like a gladiator on the pitch. We beat Italy in the World Cup! I can remember leaving the venue after the final whistle and the throngs of people out on St Stephens Green celebrating. And Dad and I stuck in the middle of it all. Everyone I talked to about Big Jack had a similar story. Memories of great times shared with people who either are no longer with us or have grown old. We have all grown old. The football and the results were nearly secondary to what people remembered. They remembered where they were and whom they were with. That is what life does to us all. That is why it is so important to have to cherish all of the moments we get in life. Because soon too they will be a memory. And we will be sad.

Sitting at his table in his apartment, looking out at the river, seeing what he saw. And it suddenly struck me. How did he fill all the hours of the day? He did not watch much TV save for the daily news and his sport. Over the last 6 months, he was not going out for walks every day. I know he read, but that still leaves many hours in the day. Maybe he wrote. Maybe he found it cathartic too. I know he did write letters to his brother. I now wonder was he terribly lonely. Did he feel alone? I tried my best to spend time with him but we all have busy lives. And when I was with him, I was always thinking about where I needed to be next. Could he sense that? I know he missed Mum and Tom. What else was he thinking about?

In his last few weeks when he was finally admitted to the hospital, his mind seemed to constantly drift back to his days at work and in particular his travels. When I was young, Dad's job had him traipsing around Eastern Europe to countries I had never heard of. Right before and right after the fall of Communism in the Eastern Bloc. He was experiencing periods of lucidity followed by deep immersions into those days. Not anxious or overly agitated, but he would get concerned about things – in particular one day he was frantic about two watches. Dad always wore a Porsche watch. There was a story about it. He had bought it on one of his trips, tempted by the label, but when he paid for it, he realised he had got the exchange rate wrong and ended up spending far more than he wanted. It was a joke we always had together. However, I did not know what he meant about a second watch. He rang me at 3:30 p.m. on a Thursday afternoon.

"My second watch. I want it back now," he said to me on the phone. No greeting, straight into it.

"Which is your second watch Dad?"

"My favourite one. The one with Tom's name on the back. It is gone. I need you to get it back for me. I need that watch back. I need my two watches" He was starting to get a bit agitated at this point, so I tried to calm him down by asking him about his day.

"Don't interrupt me." He barked. "I need my watch back. I gave it to him, and I do not know where he went or where he put it but now, I want it back. It is up to you now. You are the man of the house. You need to go there and get it back for me."

"Ok, Dad. I will get the watch back. Don't worry."

"Don't tell me to not worry. I have two watches. I have always had two watches. Just make sure you get that watch."

He ended the call soon after. I hung up and was quite distressed. His confusion was getting worse. Was this the onset of dementia? Would I ever have a proper conversation with him again?

I also had no idea what watch he was talking about. I had never heard of a watch with Tom's name on the back of it. Tom is my older brother. He died when I was younger.

I could not just call in to see Dad in hospital. COVID 19 rules meant he could have no visitors so all we could do was communicate by phone. I called the nurses' station later that day and it turned out he had been the same with all of them too. Agitated. Unsure of where he was. Something had definitely changed with him in 24 hours. He was not himself and he was not well. I casually asked the nurse on duty if he had two watches with him when he went to the hospital.

"No, I think he was only wearing one watch. He still has it on" she replied.

"Forget it, I must have misunderstood him" I replied.

I ended the call vowing to call his consultant to ensure that I could get into see him the next day.

I did not get time to make that call. Dad passed away in his sleep that night. My phone rang at 3.13 am. I had started leaving my phone on full volume at night for this very reason. Before I even looked at the screen, I knew what it was. It was a doctor from the hospital. Dad went to sleep, and he just did not wake up. He was gone.

My mind immediately went back to the last conversation I had with him. About the bloody watch. Why could he not have been more lucid? Why could we not have had a normal conversation – something nice to remember? Not ramblings about a watch that did not exist. Ending that call feeling annoyed and frustrated. I could not remember the last thing I had said to him. These are not the feelings I want to associate with Dad. I needed to put that call out of my mind and try to remember the conversation I had with him before that one.

I woke my wife to tell her what had happened. She was half awake but quickly sat up as it dawned on her. She started to cry and I hugged her. I had not cried yet. That was to come. For now, I did not know what I felt. I could not really believe what was happening. Not my dad. My dad will be around for at least another 10 years. That is what I used to tell him.

"You will see all my kids grow up, Dad – you're going nowhere."

But now he was gone. I dressed quickly, crept out of the house, and drove to the hospital. On my own. The nurse who met me at the door seemed genuinely upset when she saw me. I was ushered into a room to wait and finally, after a couple of minutes which felt like hours, a doctor came in to see me. He was quiet and in a monotone voice told me what had happened – Dad simply did not wake up from his sleep. No drama, no crash carts. He was very sick, Mantle Cell Lymphoma to be precise. Eating away at his insides. This was for the best – no suffering. Or no more suffering.

The doctor asked if I would like to see him. I nodded and followed him out the door, past the nurse's station and into a ward. There were two other beds with patients in them in the ward. Both of the occupants were awake and looking at me as I trudged by to the bed beside the window. The curtain was drawn around it.

"Help me!" shouted the patient in the bed beside Dad. However, when I looked back at him, he was smiling.

The doctor pulled opened the curtain and there, lying peacefully was Dad. He looked like he was asleep. I stood back, taking in the scene. I wanted to commit this to memory. He looked pale. I touched his hand – it was not as cold as I had expected. I noticed his watch on his wrist – the Porsche one, and I smiled. I quickly checked the other wrist but there was nothing on that apart from the hospital bracelet. No second watch Dad, I thought to myself. I leaned in, gave him a kiss on his cheek, and whispered Goodbye into his ear. I am not an overly religious or spiritual person but I could feel that

Dad had already gone. This was merely his body. His being had gone. I stood back and I sobbed quietly.

"Help Me," shouted the patient next door. I looked at Dad and laughed. He would have loved that. Breaking the tension and sadness. A priest was called from somewhere else in the hospital and as I waited for him to arrive to bless the body, I took Dad's watch off his wrist and placed it on mine. He would have wanted me to have it.

"I'll look after your watch for you, Dad." I whispered to him.

The priest arrived, said a few prayers, and then left me alone with Dad again. I did not really know what to do now. It suddenly struck me that I was the only one left out of my family now. So, I left. I gave him one last kiss on his forehead. A thank you for a lifetime of caring and generosity and fun and sadness but above all else, for just being a great Dad.

Leaving the ward, I walked past the nurse's station again and I stopped to ask what happens now. The doctor explained the process and said I could go home – Dad would be moved to the mortuary and from there the funeral director would come and get him.

And that was that. I left the hospital. I looked at my watch, well, actually Dad's watch. It was 4.53 am. Just over 12 hours since I had last spoken to him. Now I never would again.

Chapter 3

Dublin, August 2020.

Four weeks have now passed since my father died. I cannot figure out if it seems like a long time or just the blink of an eye. It is all a bit of a blur. There are moments I want to freeze in time. I want our last conversation outside of the hospital to go on longer. I want to just sit with him for one last time. I want to be able to join our last phone conversation whenever I like. Even if he was talking nonsense throughout most of it. Just to hear his voice. I want that moment when the Doctor told me he had died – bad as it was, I want to have that feeling again. I want to be able to hold his hand as I could see that his spirit had left his body, his smile and the glint in his eye gone. I want the time I spent in his apartment the very next day. Just memories and me. I want the moment I told my kids – the sadness but lack of understanding in their small faces. I want the overwhelming feelings of sadness that washed across me for those first couple of days. At the smallest thing, I would break down in tears. That does not happen now. I want to go back to writing my eulogy. How I came up with words that I needed to talk about this man's life. A feeling of satisfaction when I read it to my wife who loved it. Then the funeral itself. The nervousness I felt putting on my suit and leaving the house. Seeing my extended family at the funeral home and bizarrely travelling in a cortege through the streets he roamed in his last 4 years. And the funeral itself – my eulogy. How I managed to get through it all. How I felt I had done him proud. And the day I spent on my own in his apartment. Just me. I sat on the ground with my back to the wall and took out my phone, scrolling through videos and photos I had taken over the last 5 or 6 years. One thing was a constant in all of them – laughter. We laughed a lot. One of the things I will miss most about Dad is the nonsense conversations. Conversations about nothing at all. Calling to see him randomly and having a coffee, sitting down, and talking for half an hour. And laughing. He took such an interest in my life. In my work and in my family. Always asking me how things were going. His precious diary, which never left his side, always had all of the big events in my life written out in it. And those of my children. We wasted some years, my dad and I. But more of that later. For now, I focus on the last 10 years of our life together. When I think about my own family and my own children, I really hope I can be as good a dad to them as he was to me. That I can be as selfless and caring and generous – not only with money but with time.

Tomorrow is the last day I can go to his apartment. I do not know how I feel about that. I do not really see it as his apartment anymore, to be honest. All of his stuff is gone. It is just empty rooms. And he was only there for 4 years. But still. The memories are there and they come back to me. When it is gone and someone else is living there, it will feel so strange. I will have nowhere to go.

My mother died nearly 25 years ago. A lifetime ago now it seems. I feel like I have lived much more of my life without

28

her than with her in it. I have grown up, finished school, got a job, got married, had kids, and bought a house. Life goes on. In my eyes, Mum and Dad were soul mates. They stood for what marriage should be. I cannot remember ever hearing them have a real fight or argument. I am sure it happened, but it does not form part of my childhood memories. I spent a lot of time with my mum. I was so close to her. When I was growing up, she was my everything.

When I close my eyes and think back to my earliest memories – they are of her. One, in particular, I must have only been a toddler. I am lying down pretending to be asleep on her lap in someone's garden on a hot summer's day. Listening to her talk in hushed tones to someone nearby. It seems so vivid to me.

While I had a good relationship with my dad, I was much closer to Mum. Simply because we spent more time together. Dad was always in the background working. Mum was at home. And she played a very active role in my school life – I think she could have been at every sporting match I ever played – rugby and soccer. As I grow older and am married myself, I wonder was there tension between them. Did she resent Dad and his ability to head off on trip after trip? Seeing new places and experiencing new cultures all the time. I can remember him coming back from these trips and thrilling us all with tales of countries and cities we had never heard of. I did not know what he actually did – something about business development. Did I ever really ask? It is funny, my kids ask me all the time what I do – and I find it difficult to explain to them. Your life is one big circle – same conversations, same feelings – different positions.

I had no idea how to organize a funeral. You would think that given my experience I might have had some clue. I started by just making phone calls. Calls to family and friends telling them the news. Even saying it aloud on these calls seemed to make it more real. In one of Dad's old diaries I found the name of the funeral director who had looked after our Mum's so I gave him a call. Amazingly, he remembered me. Remembered Dad too. Passed on his condolences and then arranged to come and see me later that afternoon. I rang our local vicar – we spoke on Zoom. The funeral was set for Monday giving me the entire weekend to get ready. I needed to start thinking about what I would do with his apartment. I had a eulogy to write. In the end, I bought some beers, went home and my wife and I had one or two to celebrate his life. We told stories. We laughed. We cried.

Given COVID 19 was still in full force, the funeral was slightly different from a normal affair. It was only the immediate family, his brother and sister, and since churches were not open, held in the crematorium. I felt bad for Dad. He often wondered about who would be at his funeral. Wondering if 'so and so' would actually show up. Wondering if he would get a good send-off. I remember he was visibly shocked and emotional at the huge turnout at Mum's funeral. I think he wondered if he would get the same size. He will never know. The service itself was short. 30 minutes. It was somewhat perfect. I spoke about his life. Told some of the stories that I knew. Talked about his love of his family.

Then it was over. The curtain around the coffin slowly closed until we could no longer see it. 'Mr Bojangles' played as we all stood up, unsure of what to do. We walked out of the crematorium into the warm sunshine.

We went back to my house – we could not go anywhere else due to the restrictions – and we had a meal and a few drinks, and we told stories about Dad. It was strange. But kind of nice. His extended family.

There is a picture I have in my house of my dad and my family. It is one of my favourites. We are standing in the sunshine outside our house. Everybody is smiling –real, authentic, happy, full face beaming smiles. My Mum, my big brother and me. I reckon it was taken in 1984 – and in the forefront of the picture is Dad. With the biggest smile of all. He looks so happy. So proud of his family. I was now the only one left.

The clean-up of the apartment began the very next day. My wife, Charlotte, and I. Her job is to keep me in check. Large furniture first, struggling to see where the pieces will fit in our house. I cannot bear to see any of these pieces be thrown out or given to charity. It was different when Dad moved out of our family home and into this apartment. I knew Dad kept some things and they would be safe. But now we are the holders of the past. If it goes, it is gone for good. Once the larger bits are taken care of, we move on to the smaller things. Paintings. Pictures. It is not so much that we like the art– it is what they remind us of. It is where we used to see them hang and who used to be linked to them. I am not sure where the ones I took will end up – but I know I have to have them. Even if they stay on the floor in a spare room for a couple of years – at least I know they are there.

I took a painting of a sea scene that Dad always seemed to like. It was hanging up behind the chair he would sit in every day. I think he told me once that it came from Eastern Europe. I thought I had better keep it.

Same with lamps – and then on to picture frames and small statues. The kind that every house in Ireland would have had in the good room. The kind of stuff that nobody keeps on display anymore. Again, I feel I have to keep it. I am not an overly sentimental or emotional person but saying goodbye to somebody's things is difficult. Would we fill a St Vincent de Paul shop with this stuff? Would anyone there even want it? We eventually make it to the kitchen and the delph. This was more Mum's stuff – but again the memories attached to all these pieces. I took six Nicholas Mosse mugs – nothing says a cup of tea in my family more than a Nicholas Mosse mug. In fact, later when I had unpacked them all and put them in my cupboard, it struck me how much Dad would enjoy it the next time he was over for a coffee and he would see them all. Then I suddenly remembered why I have them. There will be no more coffees. We emptied all the cupboards. I took two tins of Baked Beans. And some bleach spray for kitchens. Ridiculous really. Waste not, want not.

From there we moved into the office. And his books. Piles and piles of books. Starting with the old-looking ones. Easy to decide to keep these. Then books on bird watching. And gardening. And Wildlife of Southern Africa. And Mrs. Beaton's guide to running a home. Then on to the novels. Dad had a habit of writing on the front page of all his books. He would write his name or his initials. This again was passed on to us. So nearly all the books in Dad's collection have something written on them.

"Dad. Happy Christmas 2013. Love, Will."

"Darling. Happy Birthday 1991. Lots of Love, James."

I cannot throw away this stuff. It's family history. In the end, I am left with a huge pile of books. Which is pointless because I do not all want them. I go through them again – being harsher this time around. I got it down to a smaller pile and moved on. It was time to go through bed linen.

I made one final trip to the apartment with my son. The smell of Dad still greets us at the door – I cannot put my finger on it though. It is not a smell of aftershave – or a smell of sickness – it is just his smell. We walk through the empty rooms one by one, holding hands. I feel my son grip my hand that little bit tighter. It is starting to make sense to him now – this is the last time we will be in his grandpa's apartment.

My son Matthew and my dad had a great relationship. Matthew is a quiet boy. Nothing would give my dad greater satisfaction than making him smile. Or having a conversation with him without me around. Because Matthew spends any time he can by my side. I see myself in him. His personality. And the way he wants to be like me. He told a boy in his class last week that his dad was Black Panther. I was so proud. Remember I said I wanted my dad to be a Superhero? I think he reminded Dad of me too. And of my brother Tom. Good memories for him.

When we walk into Dad's bedroom, a blast of emotion hits me – I am transported back years and only weeks all in an instant. To Dad lying in bed yawning. To him a short couple of weeks ago shouting out to see who was coming in through the door. To me helping him get his runners off as he made his way back to bed after trying to get up and eat something. To his obvious distress that he was not getting better. That he was so tired. That all he wanted to do was sleep. And then a memory of the last time I spent time with him in his apartment. I sat on the windowsill of his bedroom and we chatted. I cannot remember about what –it does not matter. We just talked – as we always did. And then we stopped talking. And I sat in silence and watched him. I think a bit of me knew he was very sick. A bit of me knew something bad was wrong with him. After a while, I got up to leave and saw he was also awake. He was looking at me – just as I had been looking at him. We smiled. I told him I was heading back home.

"See you tomorrow." He smiled at me.

"I love you, Dad."

"I hope so" he called out after me. And I walked out the door.

I looked in his wardrobes to check they were empty. Some bags of clothes remained – they would be dropped at the charity shop later. I jumped up to see the top shelf. Matthew laughed and asked could I lift him up to check. So, I did – I picked him up and lifted him above my head to check.

"All clear Dad." "Let's do all of them?" he asked.

So, we did. Then we moved into the office and did in there too.

"There's something up here." Matthew shouted with glee.

"What is it?" I asked.

"I don't know – it's black. I can grab it." And he pulled out a long black tube – battered and old-looking.

"Good man, Matthew, you found something important." He was grinning from ear to ear.

"Let's open it and see what's in it."

We walked into the living room and sat down on the ground. I opened the tube – there were papers rolled up like a university degree.

"What is it?"

"I don't know yet."

There were several of them. I pulled them out one by one and laid them on the floor. They were not parchments at all. They were paintings. Original paintings. Of the sea. Matthew took another look in the tube.

"There's something else in there, Dad."

I shook it out. A note.

Vilnius, 1991 m. sausio 9 d.

Mielas James

Priimkite juos kaip dovaną. Ačiū, kad patiko mano darbas. Man tai reiškia daugiau, nei tu kada nors žinosi. Palaikykite ryšį

Tavo geras draugas
Emilis.

"What does it say, Dad?" asked Matthew.

"I have no idea. Let's go home and find out".

I rolled the paintings back into the tube with the note. We took one last look around the apartment. It was empty. Matthew took my hand and we walked out the door, closing it behind us one last time.

Later, at home, I typed the words into Google translate to see what they meant. It identified the language as Lithuanian.

Vilnius, 9 January 1991

Dear James!

Take them as a gift. Thank you for enjoying my work. It means more to me than you will ever know.

Stay in touch.

Your goodfriend!
Emilis.

Chapter 4

Vilnius, 1991.

Ben and James always got off the plane last on these trips. They were not in any rush like the locals returning home all around them. Smiling at the other passengers as they tried to squeeze down the aisle, nearly pushing but not quite. Excited but fearful faces. Home again. How long has it been for many of these people? James would always give Ben his opinion on the people they saw – making up stories about where he thought they had come from and where they were going. They travelled together a lot. All over the World. A bond had developed between them at this stage. They are so comfortable in each other's company. Ben had come to learn of all James's little nuances and irregularities. How he will check his pockets at least ten times for his passport and wallet before he will get off the plane. Starting with his breast pocket in his jacket. Tap that twice. Then on to the front pockets. Then pockets in his trousers – twice for each. Finally, a check of his back pocket. How he will always have a smile for the staff – everywhere – in the Airport, taxi drivers and hotel. How he loves to talk to them all – to really find out their story and their life. How he loves his family – and talks about them at least once a day. The nervousness that comes over him going through passport control.

That nervousness is a hangover from a trip to South Africa 18 months ago. September 1989 in Jan Smuts International Airport, Johannesburg. They had just arrived on their first trip to Southern Africa and were full of excitement. James joined the passport queue first, as usual talking to all around him. It was a swelteringly hot day, which was magnified in the terminal, and there was a throng of people queuing for passport control. James and Ben had come directly from London Heathrow – three more flights had landed at nearly the exact same time resulting in long queues and added tension in the air. Apartheid was still in full swing in South Africa. Two lines – one for Blacks and one for Whites. James joined the wrong queue and Ben had simply followed in behind. James was busy talking to a large African man who was quietly regaling him with stories of Nelson Mandela and how he would soon be free. F.W De Klerk had just been sworn in as the new president of South Africa. There was an element of hope with this new president – a belief change was in the air. It was a time of political change– similar to what was happening in Eastern Europe. Perhaps this is what drew James to the attention of the police officers stationed around the queue. The queue moved slowly and the temperature seemed to rise. By the time they had reached the top of the queue, James and Ben were drenched in sweat and flustered. A police officer came from his post, casually leaning against a wall, and asked James was he ok.

"I think so" he replied with a smile. However, no smile was returned.

"Can I see your passport please?" James handed it over.

"Is he travelling with you." He pointed at the African man beside him.

"No. He is" James pointed at Ben.

"Can I see your passport too please, Sir?" the officer asked Ben who handed it over.

"Come with me please".

"We've been queuing for over an hour and have finally made it to the top. Can we not just get through?" replied James.

"Come with me now, Sir," he barked at James.

James, with Ben following close behind, trudged off, led towards a door in the wall on the other side of the terminal. It felt like the whole terminal was watching them as silence descended. Had those there seen something like this before? Inside the door was a small room – the kind you see on TV when a police interview is taking place. No windows. One table with two chairs – both table and chairs bolted to the ground.

"Wait here" barked the man.

"What the hell is going on here?" asked James as soon as the man had left.

"Let's just calm down and wait," said Ben. "It's obviously some sort of mix-up – what did you say to him?"

"I didn't say anything to the fucker."

45 minutes later two different men opened the door and walked into the room. Both smiling. "I am sorry you have been left here," said the taller of the two. He looked more senior and spoke English with a distinctly "Dutch Afrikaaner" accent.

"Can we just leave? It is baking in here and we have meetings in town to attend to. I do not know what this is about, but I am not happy. And where are our passports? The other chap took them with him," retorted James.

The smile dropped quickly from the police officer's face.

"You are here because we want you to be here. You will stay here until we say you can leave. Do you understand that?" The mood changed. Ben looked at James nervously.

"Now, what is the purpose of your visit to South Africa?" he asked as he pulled out one of the chairs and sat down, lighting a cigarette as he did.

"We are here on business."

"What kind of business is that?"

"Do we have to explain ourselves to you with no introduction as to why we are being kept in this small room?"

The man slammed his fist onto the table. James and Ben visibly jumped.

"I do not have to explain myself to you in the slightest. You are a visitor, in my Country and I am asking why you are here."

"Now, I will start again. What is the purpose of your business?"

At this point, Ben laid a hand on James's arm and politely answered the man's question. "We are working for an International Electricity Fund looking to develop Power Stations in and around Johannesburg. It is our hope we can work closely with the South African government to develop further the powerful electricity network you already have. Our papers are in order, and we have appointments set up for the next 3 days as well as hotel reservations. All is in order. We apologise if there has been any misunderstanding or disrespect – but we are simply tired after a long flight and are not used to the heat in your country. We thank you for your patience."

The man was staring at James as Ben was speaking. James looked straight ahead, refusing to make eye contact. When Ben had finished, he continued to stare, saying nothing. The silence lasted a full two minutes.

"Thank you. I hope you both have an enjoyable visit to South Africa."

Then he leaned into James's face as he spoke,

"You sir must be careful. You are not in London now. We do things differently here and you will get yourself into trouble very quickly. And the trouble is danger."

"I am not from London. I am from Dublin. In Ireland."

There was a pause.

"Ireland. Like Fergus Slattery?" said the man.

"The very same."

"Why didn't you say so? I like the Irish. At least they came to play us in Rugby back in 1981. I went to the second test in Durban. Bloody tough match. You boys should have won. Slattery was immense. Naas Botha robbed you with two drop goals."

The man's demeanour had changed entirely. James smiled back at him. He remembered the tour all right. There was outrage at home that the Irish team had travelled. Several members of the squad had publicly pulled out of the tour, refusing to travel while apartheid raged on in South Africa. His mind also cast back to 1970 when he was a young man in Dublin. And the Springboks drawing 8-8 with Ireland in front of a tiny crowd played behind barbed wire to stop protestors storming the pitch. For many around the world, the Springboks rugby team were the ultimate emblem of apartheid. There was a large anti-apartheid movement back home, if they even knew that Ben and James were undertaking this trip, they would cause a stir.

"Ja! You Irish boys are our friends! Willie John McBride at least had the balls to bring a team here this summer. Not like those Lions in 1986." The officer continued looking at James for a response.

He was talking about a combined World XV team, managed by McBride, who went to South Africa to celebrate the centenary of the South African Rugby Board earlier that summer. It was roundly condemned back home by both politicians and the public but went ahead anyway. Unlike the proposed British and Irish Lions tour of 1986 which ended up being cancelled for political reasons.

James had learned a lesson. Do not answer back. He simply shrugged his shoulders and smiled at the officer.

"Right. Irish, eh?! I will go get my colleague and he will escort you through passport control. Good day, gentlemen."

The man rose and with his silent colleague, left as quickly as he had arrived.

"What the fuck was that all about?" said James.

"Sometimes you just have to say what people want to hear James. He is right about one thing though. We are not at home. Can you keep out of trouble for this trip? This is new for us and I'm not going to be able to bail you out of every little argument you get into."

Sullenly James agreed. They remained in the stifling heat of the small room for another 45 minutes until the first police officer returned with their passports.

"Come with me, gents." He led them out of the room, and they realised the terminal was nearly empty. Only a couple of passengers remained. One of them was the large man James had been talking to. Three officers surrounded him ripping open his bags.

Ben nudged James in the back and pointed him in the way of the exit. Looking back James caught the eye of the man – his face was crumpled in despair. James smiled apologetically.

And then he was gone. Through the exit doors and out into the main terminal.

"Welcome to South Africa," snapped the officer as he closed the door.

They finally rise, as the plane is nearly empty, and make their way out of the door. Freezing air greets them. It's 9:30 a.m. on a cold winter's Tuesday in Vilnius, Lithuania. Tuesday, January 8, 1991. Smiling at the air hostess, they make their way down the steps and onto the tarmac. Following the shuffling crowd towards the terminal, Ben takes a look around. It is a cold harsh place. Several police officers are waiting outside the doors of the terminal, two with dogs and two smoking. All cradling guns and all staring at the line of passengers. He nudges James to warn him – but he has already seen them, and the nervous twitches start all over again. Eastern Europe has been this way for the two of them for these past few months. The Berlin Wall is gone. Communism is being dismantled piece by piece. What started out in Poland quickly spread to Hungary and was now turning into a movement of democracy, sweeping through the states. Mikhail Gorbachov's ideals of perestroika and glasnost reforms were firmly aimed at creating change within the Soviet Union. So much so, that in 1989 he had implicitly taken away the threat of force against other Soviet – Bloc nations such as Lithuania. But despite the sense of change, there was still a lingering, dangerous atmosphere in the air.

There were no incidents at passport control this time, and they progressed quickly through the terminal. In the arrival's hall Alex, their translator for the week's trip greets them. James quickly strikes up a conversation with the young man who is eager to reciprocate, proudly showing off his English. He brings them outside to his car, James hops in the front and Ben slides into the back seat. It is always the same.

"Welcome to Vilnius. Let's go!" shouted Alex and speeds off into traffic.

Later that evening, James and Ben meet up in the lobby of their hotel at 9:00 p.m. They are both visibly shattered after an exhausting afternoon of meetings.

"Will we just eat here in the hotel?" asked Ben.

"No. It looks terrible – let's ask that chap at reception if he can recommend anywhere local," replied James.

Approaching the desk, they are greeted by a beaming smile from Ruslan. He was there when they arrived and had brought them to their rooms.

"Hello, gentlemen. What can I help you with?"

"We are looking for somewhere to eat. Somewhere close."

"You like Lithuanian food? I know a place close by and my friend is the manager. It's very good."

James looked across at Ben and nodded.

"Let's do it – why not?"

Ruslan ran out from behind his desk and brought the two men to the front door of the hotel. He gave them directions in broken English – but they were confident they got the gist of them.

Setting off, the cold wind once again hit them. It was swirling and there were traces of snow in the air. James pulled his coat more tightly around him and followed Ben's lead down the street. The streets were quiet.

After 30 minutes, James questioned Ben.

"Are you sure you know where we are going?"

"Yes," he snapped back. "Follow me."

James shook his head and quickened his pace to catch up with Ben. He could have sworn they had been on this street before. Finally, after another 20 minutes of what felt like walking in circles, Ben proudly points to the door of the restaurant and pushes the door open. It is a small room packed full of tables and a busy crowd. All seemingly local. It feels like the entire place stops talking and eating as James and Ben come in. Utter silence. Ben stops in his tracks and almost comically, James walks into the back of him.

"Jesus, Ben! What the fuck did you do that for?"

James looked up at the waiter who was frozen like a statue at the table beside him and smiled.

"Any tables left for two hungry Irishmen?"

No response.

"Irish?" comes a voice from the back of the room.

"Yes. Irish. Looking for a good meal and we heard this was the spot."

"Well, then my friends, you have come to the right place."

The man barked orders at a couple of waiters and within moments, they had set up a new table in the corner.

"Please, gentlemen, sit. My name is Jurgis, welcome to my restaurant," as he quickly threw a tablecloth over the table.

45

"You are the gentlemen from the Hotel? My friend rang me to tell me you might be here. You took your time."

James smiled and looked at Ben. "We may have got a bit lost."

"Not a good night to get lost for many reasons. Please sit down and we will get you warmed up."

They took their seats and immediately a bottle of wine and glasses were placed before them. James quickly poured them each a glass, they toasted the owner, and both took a gulp.

"We have no menus here gentlemen – just trust us and we will feed you well." Jurgis smiled as he disappeared towards the kitchen.

What followed was a feast beyond all expectations. The level of noise in the restaurant rose quickly as the other diners seemed to relax with their new dining companions.

After the starters, there was a knock on the door. Again, the restaurant plunged into silence. Jurgis approached the door and peered out through the curtains.

He turned quickly to the room with a beaming smile. "It's Emilis!"

He opened the door and in walked a large man. He hugged the manager in a bear-like grip laughing in a loud manner. The rest of the diners clearly knew this man as they laugh along with him, and several people stand to wish him well.

"Emilis, have you eaten?"

"Not yet!"

"Lukas, another setting, please. Gentleman, you have a friend at your table!"

The large man smiled at Ben and James. James jumped up, shook his hand, and introduced the two of them.

"Do you mind if I join you?" asked the newcomer in perfect English.

"Not at all, it is we who are joining you," replied James.

Emilis sits down and at once, he and James strike up a rapport. He is intrigued by the two visitors to the restaurant and is keen to hear what they are doing in Vilnius.

The conversation continues and James expertly brings it back to Emilis. He tells them he is born and reared in Vilnius. James asks him why all the patrons in the restaurant seem on edge every time the door opens.

Emilis laughed, "Welcome to Vilnius in 1991 my friends. It is those bloody communists – they have not gone away yet you know. We declared our independence last year – March 11. A great day. But what has changed? Nothing. They do not accept it. They have us all scared – always have had us all scared. They do not want us to be meeting in groups like this – some of the people in here are what they would call subversives. You know, people looking for a change." He paused to grab a wine glass off a passing waiter.

"And change is coming here, my friend. You wait and watch. The old days are nearly gone and they know it. It is their last stand and they are digging in their heels. Jurgis here is one of us so he lets us meet here now and then to talk about plans and talk about the good old days. Most of us here were involved in *The Baltic Way*. Did you hear about that in Ireland?"

"A little," replied James.

"It was magical. A line of Balkans standing up together against those bastards. And in a peaceful manner. That is what really confused them you know, how we could just stand there linking our arms and saying nothing."

James wanted to know more. He urged Emilis to tell them more.

However, before he could begin, Jurgis was back over, calling him.

"Emilis, will you play us a song?"

"I thought you would never ask," replied Emilis already on his feet.

Emilis ambled over to the piano on the other side of the room. It is not a big piano, and he looks like a giant sitting in front of it. Then he begins to play. And he is magnificent.

Nobody speaks in the room. Nobody makes a sound. Several people have tears openly running down their faces and he plays on and on. Then just as quickly as he starts, he stops. The room is deadly silent for several beats. Before the other diners stand and clap. James quickly jumps up and follows their lead. Emilis rises from the piano with a huge smile across his face and re-joins the table, taking a large swig of wine as he does so and wiping his brow.

"I am out of practice." He laughed.

"That was unbelievable," James said. "You could be a professional."

"I am," said Emilis, laughing.

The other diners begin to cheer for Emilis to play some more.

"I need someone to sing with me. Maria?" shouts Emilis as he ambles back to the piano.

A large woman in the corner of the room blushes and gives a nod of her head. She approaches the piano and whispers something into Emilis's ear.

"He is one of the most talented people I know. Watch this – she is an opera singer. You are in for a treat now," said Jurgis as he sits in Emilis vacated seat at the table.

Emilis beings to play. Maria sings. And it is wonderful. The small restaurant transforms into an opera theatre. Emilis has his eyes closed as his fingers run up and down the keys, perfectly timed. James and Ben do not recognise the song but is clear the rest of the room do. Several of the other diners begin to sing along quietly. Jurgis is looking at his friend, smiling, eyes glistening, nodding like a proud parent.

As the song ends, the restaurant rises as one and applauds the two. The woman blushes and courtesies as Emilis stands and kisses her hand.

"More," the diners call.

"Ok, one more song. I came here to eat and drink tonight!" shouts Emilis.

"How about a song from our new friends?" Emilis looks to James and Ben. Ben quickly looks away, head down, hoping he will not have to sing but knowing what will happen next. James jumps up like a shot.

"Of course! Why not?" He walked over to Emilis. They briefly confer before Emilis laughs aloud.

"I'll try!"

He begins to play 'Piano Man' by Billy Joel and James launches into song. It is clear that this is not the first time he has performed this, patiently waiting for Emilis to catch up with his timing, and launching into the chorus, much to the delight of the restaurant. As they reach the end of the song, the entire restaurant joins in the chorus – in broken English. James finishes, bows theatrically, and sits down to applause, cheers, and hoots of laughter.

"Who knew Billy Joel was so popular in Vilnius?" he laughed to Ben.

Emilis joins them at the table, drenched in sweat but beaming from ear to ear.

"That was fun. Now let us eat and, more importantly drink! Jurgis bring some more wine over here!"

As James and Ben had already eaten, they sat back and drank the wine as Emilis launched into a full meal. As he ate, he regaled them with stories of Vilnius and of Jurgis and himself as younger men.

They had grown up together, neighbours from birth. Jurgis was always the quieter one with Emilis brasher, louder and the one more inclined to get into trouble. Ben smiled as he heard this and looked over at James who frowned back at him, clearly not seeing any similarities in their own relationship.

Chapter 5

The life Emilis described growing up in Vilnius seemed idyllic and could have been anywhere in the world. As boys, they had the freedom of the city and were always up to something. Jurgis always had a scheme or a business running to get them some money – he would make Emilis work for him but pay him so they could enjoy themselves together. As they reached their teenage years things became a bit more difficult. The Communist regime ruled over Lithuania and so the two capitalistic boys found it difficult to obey all the rules – and began to get into little bits of trouble. Nothing serious, but enough for their parents to get worried. The 'Gulag camps' was a vibrant threat in those days. Every family knew of someone who 'disappeared' – and it was from all walks of life.

Emilis always had an artistic streak and so to foster this, his parents enrolled him in some free art classes – where he discovered he had a gift. The tutor would let Emilis stay behind after the rest of the class had left to continue his work. His tutor also played the piano and after Emilis heard him play one afternoon after class, he begged him for lessons. The tutor, Ignas, finally gave in to Emilis's constant pleadings and began to give him some lessons on the side. Ignas quickly recognised he had stumbled upon serious natural talent and so applied on behalf of Emilis to take a scholarship entrance exam for the Lithuanian State Conservatoire in Vilnius. Emilis excelled at his audition and was quickly accepted on a full scholarship. This was 1962 – just at the time that Professor Leopoldas Digrys was beginning to try to reintroduce the organ into the college. The Soviet occupiers following 1944 had destroyed most of the organs in Lithuania They believed that the organ was an instrument of religious service and not in line with their communist beliefs. This was another brush with the Soviets that Emilis became involved in. Although he was quite skilled at playing the organ, he did not like it. He simply kept playing it because it seemed to infuriate the Soviets. However, piano was his first love and despite the pleadings of Digrys, Emilis eventually turned his back fully on the organ and concentrated on the piano.

At the same time, Emilis was becoming more and more engrossed with his painting. He had set up an area in his apartment for his work and spent hours staring out his window at the views of his beloved Vilnius and creating spectacular landscapes. He was not open about this work though and would never talk about it or show it to anybody. He believed his true talent was music – and he found painting more of a hobby and a welcome distraction.

In 1969, Emilis took a trip to Klaipėda with a group of friends. Klaipėda is where the Dané River meets the Baltic Sea. He had brought his painting equipment with him on the off chance he might get a morning to himself. For the previous couple of months, he had been painting waterscapes around the lakes in Vilnius and was desperate to look at the sea. He cycled his bike to Melnragė Beach, a beach recommended to him by the locals. There, began his love affair with sea painting. His friends left Klaipėda after 4 days, but Emilis stayed on. He spent hours gazing at the sea – the wonder of The Baltic Sea and its array of colours. He painted and painted – churning out hundreds of small pieces. Again, he showed them to nobody keeping them in an old satchel and when that was full, an old box. In the end, he stayed for 3 weeks. When he returned to Vilnius, his friends were intrigued as to what he had been up to. Knowing Emilis, they all assumed it was a girl. Had he fallen in love? They were right about one thing – Emilis had fallen in love, but not with a girl. He had fallen in love with the sea. It was only a matter of time before he felt the urge to return. He graduated from college and decided to head west and live by the sea for a while. He returned and settled in Klaipėda, earning money playing piano in the bars and restaurants by night, and spending his days painting.

While playing in one of his favourite spots one night, he met a waitress called Lina. Lina was a local girl who longed to live in Vilnius and so immediately became enamoured by Emilis. He was a huge man – well over 6 feet tall and big in stature – yet when he played the piano, it nearly seemed to defy physics that such large hands could produce such a calm and beautiful sound. They quickly began a romance – Lina was the first person that Emilis showed his paintings too. Not all of them mind you – he showed four of his favourites – all of the sea. She was stunned by the beauty of them and spent days and weeks trying to convince him to show them to more people or to perhaps even put on an exhibition. However, Emilis did not want to. They were his. Not for other eyes.

4 months into their relationship, Lina realised she was pregnant. She was not sure how to tell Emilis and had no idea

what his reaction would be. He seemed to live a bohemian lifestyle – not fully settled anywhere and concentrated on painting and music. However, his reaction shocked her. He roared with delight and quickly took her to their favourite bar where he tried to buy everybody he saw a drink to celebrate. His reaction surprised himself if he was honest. He had never thought about having children before. However, being with Lina made him so happy. He could only imagine having a baby with her would make him even happier. They married quickly and in due course, the baby, a son, arrived. Emilis was obsessed with Matis from the first time he laid eyes on him. He was a big strong boy and Emilis would take delight in walking him in his pram up and down the seafront in Klaipėda, stopping to talk to the familiar faces. By that time, he was known around the town – for his piano prowess as well as the fact he was such a large man and so stood out in the crowd. Standing out in the crowd was not always the best thing to happen to you in Lithuania at that time and before long, Emilis began to get the feeling he was being watched. It was nothing obvious but every now and then, he would be sure he saw the same man following him or sitting near him in a coffee shop. His political views were not that well known. Clearly, he had a sense of republicanism – after all, he had studied under Professor Digyrs in Vilnius. Emilis had not really formulated his own political views by that time. He knew, deep down, that it was not right that his country was controlled by Moscow. And as an artist, he disliked the power and control of freedom of spirit and thought imposed by Communist rule. But he did not despise the Soviets as many people did. He had learned to live alongside them. They seemed to be a part of everyday life – one that had to be endured. Moreover, he had seen what would happen to people if they stood up against them. The Gulag camps were a real threat. Not just a story to tell Matis to try to get him down to sleep.

Klaipėda had an uneasy relationship with Moscow. Upon recapturing Lithuania from the retreating Germans in 1944, the Red Army almost immediately began to commit war crimes upon the Lithuanians. In Klaipėda specifically, rape and incredible violence were prevalent and young Lithuanian men were arrested and deported, mostly to Siberia, the majority of whom would never be seen again. The general distrust arising from these events lived on in the city and Emilis became aware of it as he integrated more into the community. Everyone over a certain age had their own story of the terror inflicted by the Red Army soldiers during those times. Even more, had a relative who was 'deported' during the late 1940s. They had been singled out as members of the Union of Lithuanian Freedom Fighters, arrested, and sent away.

However, this distrust did not manifest itself into anything more severe. Their country was fundamentally changed around them, with monuments, architecture and sculptures torn down and replaced with ones dedicated to Soviet ideological, cultural, and artistic figures. As their cultural history was seemingly erased, Lithuanians got on with the more important job of survival. They took jobs in the new Soviet factories and power plants that began to spring up around the countryside.

Speaking to his new friends about these times, anger began to grow inside of Emilis. How could his beloved Lithuania be treated so poorly? A group of locals, all older than Emilis would meet in a certain coffee shop on the seafront most days. Emilis played mostly at night, so in the mornings, he would walk down with Matis, and they would sit and listen for hours on end to the stories of the Old Lithuania. Or stories of the war and how it all ended with the savagery of the Red Army. Although he did not know it, something was stirring in Emilis. Lina could see it and she began to try to discourage him from going to meet these friends. And begging him not to take little Matis. But Matis would not go anywhere without his beloved father. They were inseparable. The bond the two of them had formed was as strong as a father and son bond could be. Matis worshipped his dad. He loved nothing more than sitting on the big man's lap, as his dad would talk to his friends, just watching and playing with his toy cars for hours on end. Lina would try to get him to stay at home some mornings with her, but Matis would have none of it. He wanted to be with his dad. He would only let Emilis put him to bed at night too – always with a story from his imagination first. Emilis would take him to lands of terrible dragons and beautiful princesses, with strong, brave knights saving the day. Lina would listen from outside Matis's room some evenings and wonder who was getting more pleasure from the stories – Matis or Emilis. When the boy finally fell asleep, Emilis would give his wife a kiss and head out to play a gig at a restaurant or hotel. Always with a smile on his face. He was content – his family was perfect, and he loved his life in Klaipėda. For now.

Although settled with his new family in Klaipėda, Emilis still had strong ties to Vilnius and would frequently travel back to his home city to see family and friends. In the early 1970s on one of these trips, he became aware, through a number of his artist friends, of a movement led by Antanas Terleckas called the Lithuanian Freedom League. This movement was founded following the Helsinki accords of 1975. The accords were a non-binding agreement signed in Helsinki by all the countries of Europe (except Albania) and by the United States and Canada to try to improve relations between the Soviet Bloc and the West. The nations pledged to respect human rights and fundamental freedoms. The league saw this as an opportunity to begin the quest for freedom for Lithuania. On one of his visits to Vilnius with his family in 1977, Emilis met Terleckas at a party in one of his friends' houses. He came away inspired by the passion of the man and the belief he had that one day soon, Lithuania would be free again. Emilis kept in touch through his circle of friends – and when the idea of a magazine came about in late 1978, Emilis jumped at the chance to contribute in some way. Writing was not his forte – but Terleckas saw an opportunity to spread the reach of Vytis – his magazine – and so asked Emilis to distribute some copies around Klaipėda when the first edition came out in 1979. Emilis brought them back from Vilnius on the train and gave them to his friends in the café shops of Klaipėda to read. They all loved it. This was risky work and Emilis knew it. He kept it all to himself – not even letting Lina know what he was doing. When the second publication came out, he retraced his steps and again brought back copies, more this time, to distribute.

Four days later, as Emilis was telling Matis his bedtime story, there was a knock on their apartment door. Lina opened the door and was knocked to the floor as five men charged into the apartment. Emilis jumped up to meet the men and tried to close the door of Matis's bedroom – not wanting his son to see what was about to happen. However, the door remained open as Emilis was tackled to the floor and pinned to the ground by the men in black coats. They landed some punches and kicks on the big man as he struggled, before handcuffing him. Emilis could see Lina screaming and could see Matis crying, but he could not hear anything – all he could focus on was his son's scared face – and his eyes. Open wide in shock. His father, his hero. Why were they doing this to him?

"Matis. I will be back in a few hours. There has been a mistake. Be strong – you are the man of the house until I get back." He called out to the boy.

Matis, now 8, wiped his tears away and nodded to his dad.

Lina was sobbing on the ground as Emilis was carried out the door – four of the men required to lift the behemoth.

"What is going on, Emilis? What have you done?"

Emilis would never forget the look on her face. It was pure disappointment. She had been telling him to be careful for months – while she did not know what he was up to, she had a sense that his trips to Vilnius were not simply to catch up with old friends. All Lina cared about in the world were her husband and her son. Her perfect little family. Now her husband was being dragged away from her. She had heard stories like this before. Men taken in the middle of the night never to return. Or to return years later, broken and scarred, never the same again. Her idyllic life was in tatters. She ran to Matis and held him tightly; kissing the top of his head and telling him everything would be ok.

"Don't worry, Mum," the boy said, holding back a sob "I will look after you until Dad gets back".

He could hold it no longer and a sob wracked his little body. Lina held him even tighter. The two of them locked in a sad embrace on the floor.

Emilis was thrown into the back of a van and driven off at high speed through the streets of Klaipėda. He arrived at a police station and found himself tossed into a cell. It was freezing and wet – he sat there for what seemed like hours. His arms wrapped around his legs slowly rocking on the floor – trying to keep warm but also trying to comprehend what had just happened. While he knew what he was doing was dangerous; it had never really crossed his mind that he would be caught. Or punished. He was scared. Scared of what they would do to him but also scared for his family. He began to blink away tears as he thought of Matis. His little Matis.

Hours later, he was awoken by several men grabbing him by the arms and dragging him out of the cell. He was brought back to the van and locked in the back, next to two other men. He did not recognise either of them. A guard joined them.

"Where are we going?" asked Emilis.

The guard smiled, showing a set of black teeth.

"You will see" he laughed and turned his face the other way.

They travelled to a train station where Emilis and his two fellow prisoners were ushered onto a train. A more senior-looking guard approached them.

"You have been found guilty of treason against the Communist party. You are hereby sentenced to 5 years labour. Take them away."

Emilis felt like his world had collapsed. How could this happen? No trial. No defence. Nothing. No goodbye to his family. He struggled to break free from the guards but there were too many of them and they started to beat him with their truncheons. He fell to the ground covering his head. Thinking of Lina. Thinking of Matis. Wondering if he would ever see them again.

Chapter 6

In 1983, Emilis stepped off the train and onto the platform of the train station in Klaipėda. It had been over 4 years since he was bundled into a carriage nearly on the precise same spot. 4 years in the notorious Perm 36, over 2,500 kilometers away in Russia. Emilis had lost a lot of weight. He was a shadow of the physically dominating figure he used to be. His previous shock of black hair was now covered with strands of white. He walked with a pronounced limp as he hoisted his bag on his back and made his way to the exit. The limp came courtesy of an overzealous guard who took offence to Emilis. The labour camp was every bit as bad as he had expected. There were many days where Emilis thought he would die there. The feelings of despair as he wondered how he would ever make it home. The constant loneliness. However, he made it through. His family got him through. The thought of being here, back in Klaipėda with Lina and Matis, kept him going through all the pain. He had written hundreds of letters to Lina over the years. They became cathartic for him. He would write about everything – particularly about the life they would have together when he returned. He gave them all to the guards. Little did he know that none of them made it past the fire in the guards' room.

Emilis rounded the corner and onto the street where he lived. He could see the apartment block in the distance. It still looked the same. He began to feel nervous. What if Lina had moved? Or what if she had found someone else? He blocked those thoughts from his mind as he picked up the pace, grimacing with the pain in his leg. He reached their apartment block and climbed the stairs slowly. Finally, he reached their door. For 1,513 days, he had longed for this moment. Now it was here, he did not feel like he could take it all in. He placed his ear against the door and listened but could hear nothing.

He knocked on the door. No response. He knocked again, slightly harder. Again, no response. The door beside his opened. An elderly woman stuck her head out the door.

"Who are you?" she asked accusingly.

"I am Emilis. This is my apartment." Emilis replied trying to remember her face. "Where is Lina?"

"She has gone to pick up the child. She will be back soon. I have heard about you." As she uttered the last words, she pulled her face into a scowl and slammed the door.

Emilis smiled to himself and sat with his back against the door. He could wait for Lina and Matis – he had nowhere else to be.

He must have fallen asleep as he found himself being awoken by a little girl standing in front of him.

"Who are you?" she asked.

"I am Emilis, who are you?" replied the girl.

"I am Audra. This is my house."

"This is my house too!" Emilis replied trying to stand as he heard shuffling coming up the stairs.

Lina walked around the corner carrying three shopping bags and was struggling to get her key out of her pocket. She stopped and looked at Emilis and dropped her bags in shock, remaining rooted to the spot. Groceries spilled everywhere on the corridor.

"Audra, come here," she called. The girl ran over to Lina and grabbed her leg.

"What's wrong, Mummy?" she asked.

Emilis felt his heart breaking in his chest. He looked from Lina to the little girl and back to his wife. She looked beautiful. Slightly older and tired but still the same Lina he loved.

"Lina. I'm home." He uttered.

Lina remained where she was. One hand covered her mouth and the other gripped the little girl.

"Emilis," she mumbled. "Is it you?" She approached him slowly and then suddenly slapped him across the face. Emilis stumbled, shocked by the ferocity and power of the slap. He stood up straight and she hit him again.

"You bastard. You left us." Again and again she hit him. Emilis finally gently took her arms by the wrist and held her. He hugged her close.

"I'm sorry. I am so sorry, Lina. I'm back."

As he hugged her, he noticed the little girl was crying, watching the scene unfold. Emilis gently released Lina and turned towards Audra.

"It's ok, Audra. I know your Mummy very well."

Lina looked at Emilis and turned to the girl. "It's ok, Audra. This is your Daddy."

Emilis looked at Lina – disbelief in his eyes. "Daddy?" he asked.

"Yes, Emilis. This is your little girl".

Emilis bent down to Audra's eye level and smiled at her. "Nice to meet you, Audra. Let's help Mummy pick up her shopping."

The two of them packed the fallen groceries back into the bags as Lina opened the door.

"Where is your big brother?" Emilis asked Audra.

"My brother is with you, Daddy. In heaven." the little girl replied.

Lina froze at the door. She turned slowly to look at Emilis who was kneeling on the ground looking at her with wide eyes. A tear rolled down her face slowly.

"Oh, Emilis, you've been gone so long."

"Where is Matis, Lina?"

"Matis is gone, Emilis."

"Gone where?"

Lina knelt down on the ground with one arm around Audra and the other on Emilis's shoulder.

"Matis died 2 years ago, Emilis. He's gone."

Emilis was silent. He looked into Lina's eyes. He realised what he had thought was tiredness behind her eyes was not that at all. It was pain. And suffering. And sorrow. And hurt. He had missed it all. It was his fault. His beloved Matis. His life. He reached out and gently wiped a tear from Lina's face. He reached his arms around Audra and Lina and brought them in close for a hug. Lina began to sob. The three of them, sitting on the dirty floor of the apartment block. The elderly neighbour opened her door and peered out. She tutted and slammed the door again.

Later that evening, after dinner and with little Audra finally asleep in her bed, Emilis and Lina sat in the living room. Emilis has so many questions, but he knew he needed to let Lina tell him in his own time.

She began at the start. With Emilis being carried out of the apartment leaving herself and Matis sitting in shock. After a week, they realised he was not coming back. Nobody had heard anything. She would walk down to the seafront each morning to talk to the men in the cafes. However, they had no news. It was as if Emilis has simply vanished. Sometimes Lina thought she saw men watching her. And a car parked outside the apartment block – the same one night after night, but she could not be sure. She knew she had to get on with her life. Something else was causing her concern. She was pregnant. She had been waiting for the right moment to tell Emilis. She cried herself to sleep for nights on end wondering how she would cope without Emilis and now with the two children.

Matis was a star. He took his dad's parting words very seriously and he was acting far beyond his age as he looked after his Mum. And he was so excited at the prospect of having a little brother or sister to play with. Days turned into weeks and into months. Lina began to visibly show. A new neighbour moved in next door – Marta. A widow, she immediately took pity on her young neighbour and began to look after her. Lina was still working in her job in the restaurant and Marta would mind Matis as much as she could. Putting him to bed in the evenings. Every night she did this Matis would tell her stories of his dad, the great Emilis. Marta scoffed at these stories – what kind of a man could have left this beautiful family alone here? Matis was unabated in his love for his father. He was sure there had been a mistake and Emilis would be back any day.

"We have to make sure everything is ok when Dad gets back," he would tell Lina and Marta on a daily basis "He left me in charge, you know".

Everybody in the apartment block knew Matis. He was such a sweet boy. Now nine, he always had time for all his neighbours – particularly the elderly ones who he would help up the stairs with their shopping whenever he saw them struggling. He told them all about his dad, Emilis, and how he would be back soon. Everybody knew the devotion Matis had for his father. The elderly neighbours would wince and some even shed a tear whenever Matis left them, as they imagined what had happened to his father. They would shake their heads and think back to their own sons – either 'disappeared' or killed in the war or post-war. They would say a prayer for Emilis and his ideal of freedom for Lithuania. And vow to do all in their power to help Matis and his young mother.

Eventually, Lina had her baby. And that too was an ordeal. She woke in the middle of the night, four weeks before she was due, in agony. She called out for Matis and sent him straight next door to get Marta. Marta came running and at once sent Matis to call on Mr. Backus who had a telephone and to ring for an ambulance. Marta stayed with Matis as he watched his mother taken away. The fear he felt when Emilis was taken returned, but Marta calmed him telling him stories about his new little brother or sister and the fun they would have.

Five days later Lina returned to the apartment with Audra. Matis was immediately besotted with his little sister. Lina would walk into the living room to find him lying beside her crib telling her stories about their dad. He watched over his mother too – always willing to help her up or get her a drink.

He felt ten feet tall as he walked around their neighbourhood, himself, his mother, and his beautiful little sister, waving and saying hello to everyone he passed. And the neighbourhood was proud of him too. The three of them looked happy, despite all that had happened to them. Gifts began to arrive at their door. These people did not have much – but they knew they needed to look after one of their own who needed their help. The outpouring of goodwill shocked Lina. While she knew a few of these people, she also knew the majority of this outpouring of love was due to Matis. It made her love him even more – and this would turn to sadness as she thought about what Emilis was missing. She was beginning to come to terms with the fact that Emilis was dead. There had been no word from him or no clues from anyone as to where he had gone.

Time kept passing and soon it was time for Audra's first birthday. Matis was keen to celebrate the event and begged Lina to have a party. Lina, despite several protests, knew this was a fight she was never going to win, so abated and agreed to have a small party outside the front of their apartment block. For the special occasion, Matis had saved up some money he had received from doing chores for his neighbours and had decided to buy Audra a gift. He thought about this gift for weeks – perusing the small shops on his walk home from school. He finally decided on a music box he had found in the window of a small store, close to their apartment. However, it was just outside his price range and so the last week before the party, Matis did every chore he could think of. His neighbours caught wind of his predicament, so everyone suddenly needed their windows cleaned or shopping carried. Matis did it all with his usual smile and finally, on the day of the party, he had enough money. Lina was inside getting the food ready when Matis came bursting in.

"Mum, I'm off to buy the present! I'll be back in thirty minutes, and we can bring everything downstairs."

"Ok, Matis," replied Lina. "Be careful."

Forty minutes later, there was still no sign of Matis. Marta came over to help and Lina said she would take a quick walk down the street to see if she could find him. She set off, smiling, and waving at the neighbours who had begun to congregate for the party.

There was no sign of Matis near their apartment, so she continued further down the street. Her attention was drawn to a commotion further down the street. There was a car up on the pavement, a crowd of people had gathered around as an ambulance and the police tried to deal with the crash. Lina felt a shiver down her spine as a sense of dread suddenly overtook her. She hurried to the scene, pushing past onlookers. The car had mounted the pavement and crashed into the wall of a row of buildings. There was a man sitting on the footpath, with his head in his hands sobbing uncontrollably. Two police officers were by his side, talking loudly at him asking questions. Lina could see two ambulance men who had lifted a body onto a stretcher. The body was small. It was not an adult. Lina's heart stopped. Everything happened in slow motion as she approached the stretcher. A police man tried to hold her back, but she pushed him out of her way. She got to the stretcher just as the paramedic was trying to cover the face of the body with a sheet. It was Matis. Little Matis. She felt arms grab her and pull her away, but she fought them off. She could hear an awful sound – it sounded like a wail from an animal. She realised it was coming from herself.

Matis had been on his way home, music box delicately wrapped in his hand when the car lost control and mounted the footpath. It slammed him against the wall. It took six men who arrived quickly at the scene to pull the car off him. Onlookers said he died instantly. His small body had been crushed. However, his face was untouched. So, when Lina saw him later at the morgue, it looked like he was merely asleep. Her little Matis. Her precious little boy who had looked after her so well. She kissed him on the head and hugged him, whispering into his ear "I love you, Matis. I will see you again. You were so loved, and your father loved you even more than me. I hope you see him again now. Wait for me and Audra, we will join you later."

It gave her solace to think that somewhere, Emilis was minding her little boy. And that Matis was finally reunited with his hero.

Matis's funeral was enormous. It felt like all of Klaipėda showed up to pay tribute to the boy. People who did not know Matis or the family that well, remarked how visibly upset the older crowd at the funeral were. There was a sense of disbelief that such a tragedy could happen to the family – especially following the disappearance of Emilis. If it were not for Audra, Lina would have found it hard to continue to live. First Emilis and now Matis. Ripped away from her. But the little girl was so young and oblivious to the pain and suffering all around her that she provided such joy to Lina. Marta too was a column of strength for Lina. She appeared to be a cold, hard woman, but that was merely her exterior appearance. Inside she was a kind, caring soul who cried herself to sleep most nights thinking of poor Matis. There was a terrible sense of loss throughout the entire neighbourhood for months after the accident. Then, as it is prone to do, life goes on.

Lina and Audra coped. They had each other. After a couple of months of never letting the girl out of her sight, Lina eventually went back to work, with Marta helping and looking after Audra whenever needed. Life began to get back to normal.

That is until Lina came home from shopping to find Emilis at her door.

Emilis listened to the story in utter silence. Tears rolled down his face. When he thought back to his lowest moments in the camp, the one thing that kept him going was his family. And in particular, his Matis. He was his everything. He would spend hours thinking about how he was growing up, what he was learning in school, what sports he would like to play, what kind of a man he would become. And now all that was gone. There is something very wrong about a parent outliving their child. It freezes the child in time – Matis will never be more than 8 years old in Emilis mind.

He also felt a huge degree of shame. Why had he risked it all for a stupid newspaper? That had made no difference whatsoever. Everything was still the same in Lithuania. Would he have been able to help Matis if he was around? Probably not. It was a freak accident. But that did not change things. He had missed 3 years of his boy's life – indeed, the last 3 years of his boys' life. And the solace given to Lina that Emilis was somehow looking after Matis in heaven was also untrue.

He had so many hopes and dreams for his little boy. But most of all he longed to spend time with him again. Like the time they had together before he was taken away. Walks down to the seafront – coffee and a bun at the café with Matis happily playing with his toy cars while Emilis talked. The stories he would make up for Matis at bedtime. Watching his boy sleep, his peaceful face. Or when he would have a nightmare, hearing the gentle padding of his feet, as he would come into his parent's room looking for Emilis to make it all go away.

The next day, Lina took Emilis to see Matis's grave. It was a simple headstone in a busy graveyard. Lina and Emilis sat beside it, holding on to each other but not speaking for over an hour. Complete silence as they both dealt with their grief- Emilis' new but Linas' old and coming back to her in waves and with the same pain. Afterwards, on the walk home, Emilis stopped in the street and turned to Lina.

"I am so sorry, Lina. I am so sorry I was not here. I am so sorry that I was taken away. I am so sorry Matis is gone. I will make it up to you if you give me a chance. With Audra. We can become a family again."

Lina looked into his eyes – the eyes of the man she loved. She remembered all the times she had cursed him over the last four years. The pain and heartache she had suffered when she thought he was dead. And now he here was standing in front of her. She kissed him and replied.

"Of course, Emilis. I love you. We are a family."

They held hands and walked back toward their home. Back towards Audra and a new life.

Emilis had noticed that when he walked from the train station home, he could see two men following him. They were not even trying to blend into the crowd. They wanted him to know that they were watching him. He also saw the black car

71

outside the apartment block when he arrived. Again, no hint of trying to hide.

Chapter 7

Meath, 1985.

It was a cold winter's Saturday at the end of November. Bitterly cold. My family were at home for the morning. My big brother, Tom and I, aged nine and five, were inside playing. Tom would always choose the games in these situations, and I would happily follow along after him. I worshipped him. We were boisterous boys. Not wild or out of control but if there was an opportunity for a bit of wrestling or tackling in a game, we were all over it. That morning we had been playing Superheroes. I was always Spiderman, and my brother Tom was always Batman. We would be on the same team – trying to defeat the imaginary bad guys that would pop up around the house. My Mum and Dad would happily let us play like this for hours on end. As a father now, I understand this inherently. Relevant peace and quiet.

That particular morning, something happened in our game that caused a big fight. I do not recall why or how it started but I know it ended with Tom hitting me – a full, proper punch on my jaw. I was stunned. I distinctly remember standing there in utter shock. He had never done that to me before. It was sore sure, but it was the feeling of disbelief that I remember most. Tears welled up in my eyes immediately.

Tom, knowing what he had done, and probably knowing the roaring that was coming, quickly put his arms around me and started apologising profusely. However, it was too late. My tears and screaming came together. I was trying to push him off me, to run and find my mum, but he was holding me back and covering my mouth. Mum and Dad heard the commotion, and both came running up the stairs. I ran to Mum and told her exactly what had happened. Tom was standing there, sheepishly shuffling his feet and looking scared. Mum picked me up and brought me away and as I looked over her shoulder, I could see Dad approach Tom, raising his voice.

Mum brought me downstairs, calmed me down and gave me some biscuits to cheer me up. I could hear Dad shouting at Tom upstairs. Inside, I was smiling. It was usually me who got in the most trouble in our house, and now, here I was, sitting in the warm kitchen with Mum, eating biscuits and listening to Tom getting into trouble. Life was good. Tom was sent to his room for the rest of the day. Dad came down and ruffled my hair. I was getting so much attention. I asked if I could watch some TV – and I was allowed! That never happened!

A couple of hours later, after a lunch without Tom, I crept upstairs and quietly knocked on the door of our room. He let me in, and I sat down on my bed – the lower bunk. He had been crying – he had those blotches on his face that can only be caused by prolonged crying.

"I'm so sorry, Will. I didn't mean it," he said.

"It's fine. I got biscuits. And got to watch TV. Anyway, it didn't really hurt," I replied grinning.

Tom smiled at me and gave me a hug. He was always doing that. He was such a caring boy.

"How long do you have to stay in here?" I asked him.

"Dad said he will come and get me later. We have to go and see our cousins for dinner remember?"

I had forgotten. Our cousins lived about half an hour away in Dublin. We hated going to see them. They were all older than us – even older than Tom – and did not really pay us much attention.

"Pity you couldn't get grounded for that," I smiled.

Tom agreed. We were back friends.

"Sorry I screamed and got you in trouble Tom."

"It's ok. I deserved it." '

Dad finally let him out of his room later that afternoon and we played Lego on the floor of the kitchen. It was the warmest room in the house with a large stove. The temperature had not improved outside, and Tom and I were secretly hoping we would not have to make the trip to see our cousins. But sure enough, at 5 p.m., Mum rounded us up and made us get changed into our 'nice' clothes. She ran the tap in the bathroom and tried to smooth down our hair and clean our faces.

"Do we really have to go, Mum?" I asked.

"Yes, darling. We do not see them very much and you know it makes your dad happy. We will not stay late because it is set to freeze hard tonight. We will be back home soon" she replied.

We set off at 5:30 p.m. Dad had to sit in the car for a while before we got in, with the heating on full blast to try to clear the windscreen of ice. He had already poured warm water on it, but it was almost frozen solid again. Mum had checked with him whether it was too bad to drive.

"It's not that bad. Let's just go now and come back early." Dad said.

We set off. Dad was playing his Billy Joel tape in the car as usual, and we were all singing along at the top of our lungs.

We seemed to spend a lot of time in that car as a family. Holidays were always spent in Ireland, driving everywhere. Tom and I in the back of the car, Dad always driving and playing music, Mum in the passenger seat talking to both Dad and us simultaneously it seemed, and always quick with a snack of some sort to stop us from making a fuss. Other trips I can remember, coming home from places late at night. Trips to cousins I suppose. I would pretend to be asleep in the back; I loved the feeling of darkness outside, trying to guess where we were on the trip by the turns in the road. Listening to Mum and Dad talking and laughing. And Tom snoring.

There is a dangerous bend about halfway through the trip. Dad slowed right down to make it, but even at that, the back of the car fishtailed slightly as we went around the corner.

Tom and I shrieked with delight in the back. Dad swore but got the car back under control and we set off again.

"Just going to take it nice and slowly" Dad smiled across at Mum who was gripping the sides of her seat. "They won't mind if we are a little bit late".

I do not know exactly what happened with the crash. I know Tom and I were in the back talking and laughing. I know Mum was half turned in her seat, joining in. Dad maintains the light was green and the other car went through a red light. That makes sense as the other driver was drunk. However, a witness stated that our light was orange, if not red, and that Dad accelerated through the crossing.

I can remember the impact. It came out of nowhere. Not on my side of the car. On Tom's side. Then I remember nothing. The next thing I knew I was in an ambulance.

My Uncle Joe is a doctor. He was working that evening and was racing home to try to be there when we arrived. He came across the accident 10 minutes from his door. There were flashing lights all around as an ambulance and a police car were on the scene. Joe quickly pulled in and jumped out of the car, as a doctor willing to help. It was only as he approached the vehicles, he recognised the car. Our car was in a bad way; it had been pushed over at an odd angle against the wall on the far side of the road. Another car was near, the front severely damaged – it looked as if it had been just pulled out of our car. Dad was sitting on the steps of the back of the ambulance. He had blood flowing from a cut on his head, but he was manically trying to push the paramedic, trying to attend to him, away.

"Where are my boys?" he cried seeing Joe.

"I'll go find them," Joe called back.

Joe ran over to the scene. He saw Mum being lifted out of the passenger seat. She was not moving. He stood back to let firemen through who had also just arrived at the scene.

"We need to cut open the back," cried one of the paramedics. "There are 2 boys in there and I'm not sure what we are dealing with."

When they finally cut the roof of the car, 20 minutes later, they found Tom lying on top of me. Protecting me. Nobody knows when exactly he stopped breathing. However, it was clear he was alive for some time following the initial impact. He was thrown sideways with the impact on his side of our car, and whether he was actually trying to protect me, or whether it was just gravity, it is an image that anyone there that night will not forget. A 9-year-old boy covering his 5-year-old little brother. The ultimate Superhero.

They took his body off me and found me sobbing to myself, shivering from both the shock and the freezing temperatures. I was taken to the ambulance, and then to the hospital quickly. I had no injuries, bar a couple of scrapes, but my body temperature was dangerously low. I had to stay in hospital for 2 nights, blissfully unaware of what had happened.

Mum was in the hospital for 3 weeks. She had shattered her left leg and had some internal bleeding. She would always walk with a limp to further remind her of that day. As if she needed it. Dad was like me, a nasty cut on his head but apart from that, he was fine.

I found out that Tom was dead the day that I returned home from the hospital. My dad and my aunt told me about the accident. I was numb. I did not cry. I simply nodded and then asked if I could go outside and play.

We were a perfect little family. I know it is probably rose-tinted glasses but we always seemed happy. Yes, Dad travelled a good bit with work, but when he was around, he was lots of fun. Always doing something – whether it be out in the garden or something in the house. Something that Tom and I could 'help' with. And Mum. Mum was everything to us boys. We adored her. We would sit for hours with her, as she cleaned up, cooked us dinner, or played with us.

Something had changed inside Mum after she came back from the hospital. Not because of her injuries but something had changed in her since Tom died. She looked sad. No, that is not true. She looked like she was trying to hide her sadness all the time. She would go around the house putting up pictures of Tom. It felt like we were living with a ghost. And even though she tried to hide it from me, Mum cried. A lot. I would lie in my bed, a single bed now as Mum got rid of the bunk beds as soon as she came home, and could hear sobbing coming from her bedroom.

I simply missed my big brother. I missed having someone to play with. I missed having someone to get the bus to school with. Or to laugh at cartoons with. His presence was everywhere. Lots of my clothes were hand-me-downs from Tom. And the toys I played with, the footballs I kicked, they all reminded me of him. I could not watch a Batman cartoon anymore without feeling terrible. I became more and more withdrawn. I had never been the chatty, sociable one – that was Tom – but I went deeper and deeper into my shell. And Mum and Dad did not seem to notice. They were busy trying to get on with their lives. Trying to wake up every morning and not immediately mourn the loss of their darling boy. A boy with his whole life ahead of him. We had to find a way to keep going with our lives. To live as Tom could not. We kept on with the mundane trudge of life, work, school, homework. Just without much of the laughter that was there before. And I knew we would all think of Tom all the time.

Losing a child must be one of the worst things imaginable to happen to any parent. But it is also an awful thing to happen to siblings left behind. I always felt that I was battling for attention against Tom. And that is a hard battle to win as he was never going to do anything wrong ever again. And I could not express these feelings out loud. Imagine how my parents would have felt if they thought I was resentful about my dead brother. The boy who protected me from the crash and perhaps gave his life for mine?

Time passed and we survived and learned to live as our new family. I eventually turned 9 years old. The same age as Tom was, and always would be. Sometimes I would catch Mum looking at me and I could swear she was comparing me to Tom. I was a bit smaller, not as good in school and definitely not as good at sport. Nevertheless, I know my parents loved me. There would be times when we would all momentarily forget about our tragedy, and these were my favourite memories of this part of my childhood. It gave me a glimpse of what life might have been like had it not been for that fateful day; that car hitting the side of ours and ending it all.

School was not going particularly well for me. I was a clever boy, but I just did not have the attention span to deal with school. I wanted to be outside all of the time. I was also very shy which made it difficult for me to make many friends. School reminded me of Tom constantly. It was a small national school and there were pictures of Tom on some of the walls. I much preferred being at home with Mum. Dad too, but he was away a lot with work and always seemed quite distant when he was around.

The summer holidays were magic. Two whole months at home. With Mum to myself. We would pack in as much as we could, taking little trips around the country, Dad joining us when he could. It felt like we were back to where we had been before. Happy. We would never forget Tom and he would always be a part of our family. But we did not all die that day. It was up to us to live our lives to the full for Tom's sake. I definitely felt that. As I turned 10 and was older than he would ever be, I felt him on my shoulder. I felt that everything I did was for the two of us. Not in a sad or pressure-inducing way. In a happy way. He was my big brother, and I will always love him.

Chapter 8

Vilnius, 1991.

Ben and James had a free morning the next day with no meetings planned. At some point the previous night, Emilis had got wind of this and decided he would show Ben and James around his beloved Vilnius. The next morning at 9 a.m. on the dot, Emilis arrived at the hotel to collect them. However, when Ben woke up, he was not feeling well and rang through to James's room to tell him he was going to skip the tour and try to sleep it off. James was happy enough to carry on without his colleague and met Emilis in the lobby.

"Let's go see Vilnius," laughed Emilis and they set off. They walked and walked through the streets of the old city. He showed James all of the historical sites. They talked non-stop. They both shared a love of art and music and this commonality meant they had lots to talk about. His new friend intrigued James. Despite his towering physical appearance, he was a gentle man with a vast knowledge of the arts and history of Vilnius.

They also talked about their families. Emilis told James all about Audra. And about Matis. James told Emilis all about his sons Tom and Will. About how Tom was also taken from him. His beloved Tom. And Will, now 11 and at home.

Neither man had ever spoken to someone else who had also lost a child at a similar age before. They felt an immediate sense of kinship, a freedom to really talk about how they felt. They lamented about how neither would get to see their boy grow up – get to see all the mistakes, happiness, and disappointments he would encounter in his life. They talked about the difficulty of losing a child and the feeling of being unable to grieve fully as they needed to be strong for their family. For their other child, still very much alive. The awful sense of resentment they sometimes felt when they look at their surviving child. And then the shame and embarrassment they would feel for even having those thoughts in the first place. They also felt a sense of guilt. James talked about how he thinks about the traffic light every day, how he is sure, it was green. Emilis similarly talked about not being there for Matis. Not being around to protect him.

They felt an incredible sense of mutual understanding over their loss, bringing them very close in those few short hours together.

They talked about the world they wanted Audra and Will to live in. The difficulties that they had both encountered in life and how all they wished for their family was peace and security. They talked and walked for hours, bonding over heartbreak.

As Emilis dropped James back to the hotel, he invited his friend to his apartment for a bite to eat, later that evening. James was quick to decline but Emilis assured him that Lina would be delighted and would prepare something special. James politely agreed and would see his friend later. He would try to get Ben to come too.

Emilis came back to the hotel that evening to pick them up. Despite being able to attend the meetings they had for the afternoon; Ben was still feeling shattered and so decided to stay at the hotel. So, James and Emilis set off on foot together in the direction of the apartment block.

Lina met them at the door. James was struck at once at how pretty she was. She spoke little English but made James feel welcome with warm smiles and gestures. She ushered them into the living room where she sat them down and fetched them both a cold beer. Emilis was visibly settled and happy in his surroundings. Lina quite obviously doted on him, and a beautiful smell was emanating from the kitchen.

"Proper Lithuanian homecooked food for you," Emilis told him. "Enough for Ben too so you will have to eat double." He laughed.

The door opened and a beautiful girl entered the room.

"James, this is Audra, my daughter."

"Delighted to meet you," said James.

Audra smiled and softly said hello. "Audra is fluent in English too – she is in school here in Vilnius and is a great scholar." The pride for his daughter exuded from Emilis.

"I have a son just your age," said James. "He is also in school – not sure if he's a great scholar but he seems to be having fun!"

Lina called for Emilis from the kitchen, and he jumped up to help. While he was gone, James's eyes were drawn to the photos in picture frames scattered around the room. Several of them were of a smiling young boy.

"That's Matis," said Audra. "My brother. He died when I was a baby."

"He looks so happy," commented James.

"He was," said Emilis from the door. "That's my memory of him. Smiling and laughing," His eyes glistened as he spoke of the boy and Audra went to his side and squeezed his arm.

"Lina is ready for us – let's eat," smiled Emilis.

From a small kitchen in their apartment, Lina produced a mountain of food. Emilis kept the beer and wine flowing steadily and after a couple of hours, James was full to bursting point but very content. Emilis suggested they move back to the living room to relax and James happily obliged. They sat down and Audra and Lina joined them. Throughout the meal, James and Emilis had kept up a constant conversation on art.

"You have to show him your paintings, Dad," urged Audra at one point.

"We will see," replied Emilis. This was his standard response about his art.

As they sat in the Living room to relax, Audra started again – "Come on, Dad, show him".

"Ok, I'll go and get a couple" Emilis left the room.

Audra turned to James "I am always trying to get him to show these paintings– he will not show them to anyone outside of the family and I think he could sell them easily at an exhibition".

Emilis returned with four scrolls under his arm. He used the wall of the living room as a show space, unrolling the four paintings, and sticking them to the wall. James was gobsmacked. He was looking at four of the finest oil paintings of the sea he had ever seen in the flesh. They looked so real, he thought for a moment that they were photographs.

"Emilis. These are unbelievable. Why have you these hidden away. People need to see these." He spoke as he stood to get a closer look.

They were all of the Baltic Sea, all done during his time in Klaipėda. The detail in each was breathtaking. The colours of the sea – James could nearly feel the cold spray from the waves the closer he got to the painting.

Emilis smiled with pride as James showered him with compliments. Still, he was not convinced to show them.

"These are mine," he explained, "They are for me and my family. To remind us of a time past in Klaipėda. I do not paint anymore you know."

"Why ever not?" exclaimed James.

"Those days are gone now. In the past. When I returned, I tried to pick up a brush, but the joy had gone from the experience. Painting used to be my escape, my relaxation. However, when I returned and tried to paint again, I was hit with all the emotions of that time. And I was sad that those days had gone. So, I don't do it anymore."

Emilis began to talk of the time after Matis had passed away. Emilis began to settle back into life in Klaipėda. It took a lot of charming and, but even Marta next door began to warm to the big man. He would take Audra for walks, just as he had with Matis, down to the seafront and he would stand and simply gaze into the sea. His old friends from the cafes kept their distance. It was clear that Emilis had been identified as a troublemaker and nobody wanted to be seen with him. He called into the old restaurants and hotels he used to play the piano in and looked for some work but was politely declined everywhere he turned. He was blacklisted. He could still sense that he was being watched. Lina was working hard, trying to earn as much as possible to provide for the family. However, she was tired and felt she was missing spending time with

Audra. They sat down one night and talked about leaving Klaipėda.

"Where would we go?" asked Lina. She had never lived anywhere else.

"Vilnius," replied Emilis. "I still have friends there. We can get set up with an apartment and I will get some work. It will be a new start," he promised.

"Emilis. Promise me no more trouble. I can't take any more of it and I can't face losing you again."

He looked into her eyes and promised. "Those days are behind us now Lina. It is the three of us now, you, Audra, and me. We will be better off in Vilnius, I promise."

Three months later, they had settled in Vilnius. They had found a nice apartment, Emilis had picked up a regular gig at a couple of hotels, and his friends and contacts in his alma mater had set him up with a few piano teaching jobs to help pay the rent. His leg meant he could not do any physical work, which was a shame as another friend had a construction business and was crying out for an extra pair of hands. Lina decided not to work – she stayed at home with Audra. She knew nobody in Vilnius and Emilis would race home from work to be with the two of them. His old circle of friends were good to them, particularly Jurgis. They would encourage their wives to look out for Lina and before long, she had formed a small set of friends with children of similar age to Audra. Life was getting back to normal for all of them.

And life continued to be good to them. Audra started school and loved it. This also gave Lina some more free time, and she took on a parttime job in a café. Emilis was excelling at teaching, something he had never tried before. He came to the attention of the University who were always on the lookout for talented, inspiring lecturers for their music programme. Emilis was delighted and honoured to be considered and jumped at the chance to interview. He easily got the job and so began a lecturing career that would last for many years.

Emilis and Lina discussed the possibility of growing their family. However, after two years of trying, with two miscarriages, they decided it was not to be for them. They were thankful that they had a family of three and Audra was growing up to be a beautiful and kind child. She excelled at school. She was a different personality from Matis. Quieter and happier in the background reading a book, yet she had the same charm to her.

Audra felt a strong bond with her brother Matis. His photos were dotted all over their apartment and she would often hear her mother, but more so, her father talk of him. She felt an uneasy pang of jealousy at times. It was clear from how he spoke of Matis that her father worshipped the little boy. Audra wanted more than anything to have her father feel the same about her. But it was difficult for her. She was here, living. And Matis was gone. He could never do anything to get into trouble now. And whilst it did not happen often, she could. She sometimes felt she had to try extra hard for her father's attention, extra hard for his adulation. Perhaps this was why she studied so hard at school. She enjoyed it of course but she always wanted to excel in any tests so she could run home to Emilis and show him her results.

The reality was that there was no competition in Emilis' mind over his two children. He loved them both equally. In different ways. Matis, as his first-born and son, would always have a special place in his heart. The fact that he was gone, taken from him when he was incarcerated, also made this connection and bond even stronger.

However, Audra was his little princess. For the first couple of months, after he returned, every day spent with her would teach him something new about her. The way she would cry, the stories she liked. A smile from her was worth more than Emilis could imagine. And she was so clever! His chest bulged with pride every time she would come home from school with another amazing test score. He could see so many of Lina's traits coming out in her. Her attention to detail. The frown she would have on her face when she was really concentrating on something. She would hum when she was reading a book – something Emilis would constantly tease her about. And she was caring. He had never seen such a caring child. Always looking out for her mother and always looking out for her friends.

As evening turned into night, Lina and Audra left the two men looking at the art, sitting having a drink and talking.

"You never told me about Baltic Way. I've heard of this being mentioned a lot – but I don't really know what it was," remarked James.

Emilis jumped up and grabbed the bottle of whiskey they were drinking and topped up both glasses.

"We will need a bit for this story!" He smiled.

He settled back into his chair and began to tell the tale.

"James, in order for me to tell you about The Baltic Way, I need to give you a little history lesson first. On August 23 1939, an agreement was signed in secret in Moscow. This agreement, known as the Hitler-Stalin Pact or also the Molotov-Ribbentrop Pact after the 2 men who signed it, let the Soviet Union occupy Estonia, Latvia and Lithuania (the

Baltic States) in 1940. The Soviet Union denied the existence of this pact – they claimed that the Baltic states had simply joined the Union voluntarily. In 1941, the Nazis, under Operation Barbarossa, took back these states. Initially we Lithuanians were happy – we felt the Nazis were liberating us from the Soviet occupation. In fact, we even set up a provisional government as we seemed to think the Germans would simply reestablish our independent state. This didn't happen. We suffered for almost 4 years. Then, as the war was ending, the Soviets arrived back and took back control of all 3 states. We were back where we started. And nobody seemed to care."

Emilis stopped and took a large swallow of his whiskey. James was enthralled by the passion his friend spoke with. Emilis continued;

"Many years passed. The Molotov-Ribbentrop pact was continuously denied by the Soviets. By doing this they kept their control over us. As we approached the 50th anniversary of the signing of the pact, there was a change in the air. You could feel it here in Vilnius. In 1986, we heard of Black Ribbon days being held across Western cities. These were protests at the human rights violations taking place by the Soviet Union. The following year, we held one of these protests ourselves, here in Vilnius, at the monument to Matthew Mickiewicz, the poet. A group of us got together – you met most of them at the restaurant – and cautiously made our way there to join in. A crowd of at least 3,000 had gathered – far more than we could have imagined. While the Soviets were there watching, there was no trouble. We received word through our friends that a huge protest was planned for August 23, 1989 – the 50th Anniversary. It would involve thousands of us. There were rumours that the Estoninas and Latvians were involved too but nobody was sure. The city was alive with excitement and anticipation. We met nightly in the restaurant, Jurgis filling us in on all the gossip he had picked up during the day. In early July, a man from the Sąjūdis came to see us." Emilis paused as he saw the confusion on James's face.

"It means 'The Movement.' The Sąjūdis is a group set up with the goal of politically, winning back independence for Lithuania. They are basically saying out loud what so many of us have been thinking for all of these years." James nodded and Emilis got back to his story, taking the opportunity for another quick swig from his glass.

"They, along with their counterparts in Estonia and Latvia were organising the event. I could not believe how much traction this had gained. Something magical was taking place, something I never thought I would see in my lifetime. A peaceful protest, a unification of our Baltic States. The man from the Sąjūdis told us that we were to hold hands – and that a line of people was to stretch from right here in Vilnius all the way to Tallinn in Estonia. I do not know where the idea for a human chain came from. I don't think anybody really knows – it's one of those things in history now that everybody claims to be in the room when it happened. The Estonians claim they came up with the idea. Who knows? Later that month the Sąjūdis addressed the nation calling all Lithuanians to attend."

"At the same time, a man called Romualdas Ozolas, I knew him from my university circles, started collecting signatures around the country calling for the withdrawal of the Red Army from Lithuania. He gained over 2 million signatures. There was something special happening. The 23rd of August was a Wednesday. We would need to take time off work. Some employers let their staff take the day off but for others, they simply would not turn up."

Emilis took another break and another drink. He was as animated as James had seen him.

"The night before the event, a large rally was planned in Vilnius Mountain Park. Thousands of us attended and watched in awe as the Sąjūdis demanded the denunciation of the Molotov – Ribbentrop pact and the restoration of Lithuanias' independence! I had never seen anyting like it. The next day, the protest was set to commence at 7:00 p.m. but the city was alive well before then. It seemed like all of Vilnius was on the move. We had been briefed by Jurgis that we were to go to Cathderal Sqaure, right here in the centre of Vilnius. Remember we visited there this morning? The start of the line was to be at the tower of Gediminas Castle. During the day, planes flew overhead, apparently coordinating the events. There was talk of huge traffic jams all over the country. It was such a time to be alive James! The excitement in the air. At exactly 7:00 p.m., bells tolled in unison on the radios that we all had with us. We all grabbed hands, facing West – the direction of Tallinn. Flowers were dropped by an airplane overhead. We lit candles. We flew flags. We cried tears of sadness and joy. It was the greatest day of my life James."

Emilis sat back, drained by the telling of the story. James was silent. He was thinking of what he knew of the time. Watching from a far, the entire West was blown away by the peaceful and symbolic display from the Balkans. It was thought that over 2 million people lined the route. 1 million of them in Lithuania alone. The population of Lithuania at the time was only about 3.7 million people. He could recall the video footage taken from the skies above showing an unbroken line of people stretching out for miles.

The two men sat in silence for a couple of minutes, deep in thought. Finally, James spoke:

"Your paintings really are extraordinary, Emilis. People deserve to see them. Lithuanians deserve to see how beautiful they are." James pleaded with Emilis.

"No! They are for me and my family."

Emilis stood up and walked over to the wall where the paintings were. He looked at them all and then turned on his heel and left the room. James was concerned he had upset his new friend, but moments later Emilis returned, smiling carrying a long thin tube under his arm.

"They are for my family. And now, for you, James." He rolled up the four paintings carefully and slid them into the tube. He quickly scribbled something on a note and pushed it in too.

"These are for you."

"Emilis. Do not be so stupid. I cannot take them. They are yours."

"Enough! They are a present for you. However, keep them for you and your family. Please do not sell them or put them in an exhibition. These are personal."

"I really can't take them." Pleaded James.

"You will and you have to," said Emilis smiling.

"Very well. But I must give you something in return." James took his watch off his wrist.

"This is a special watch. It is engraved with Tom's name on the back. I bought it when he was born. If you insist on giving these to me, you must take my watch. And if we change our minds, we will have to meet up to make an exchange again."

Emilis laughed, "I love that idea. Something special for me and something special for you. James, I will take care of this watch with my life. And we will meet up again soon and I will give it back to you."

The two friends embraced, slightly unsteady on their feet after the whiskey. The door opened and Lina came in speaking sharply to Emilis.

"What did she say?" asked James.

"She told us that we are drunk and mad and must go to bed before we wake up Audra and the rest of the apartment block" laughed Emilis.

"She also told me to tell you that she will make sure I take care of your watch!" he laughed loudly, drawing a playful slap from his wife.

Chapter 9

The next day was Friday, January 11. It started again as a very cold day in Vilnius. James woke up with a splitting headache in his hotel room to the sound of someone knocking on his door. It was Ben.

"How are you feeling?" grinned Ben as he entered the room.

"Bloody awful. What time is it?"

"10:30 – you've missed breakfast! We have a meeting in an hour and a half so get ready. Here take these" Ben threw a couple of paracetamols across to James.

"Ok. See you in reception in 30," James closed the door and walked into the bathroom. He jumped in the shower and tried to get his head straight for the meetings. He subconsciously rubbed his wrist and realised his watch was not there. He smiled as he remembered where it was. Drying himself with a towel, he walked back into the room and spotted the black tube with the paintings in it. He unfurled them and laid them out on his bed – they really were magnificent. He carefully placed them all back in the tube, certain that he must meet Emilis later and exchange them for his watch.

The two men decided to walk the short distance to the offices where their meeting was being held. James turned up his collar at the bitter wind blowing into their faces but started to feel a bit better after gulping in some of the air.

"How are you feeling today, Ben?" he asked.

"Not great. But I feel better than you look!" his friend replied.

As they arrived at the meeting for their midday meeting, there was a commotion in the reception area. Their interpreter, Alex, ran over to meet them.

"Gentlemen, how are you. There is a bit of drama unfolding here in Vilnius," he exclaimed.

"Soviet military units have seized the National Defence Department building!" he continued.

James and Ben glanced nervously at each other. This had always been their greatest fear travelling around Eastern Europe. While it was clear that some sort of Soviet breakup would occur eventually, they knew there was always the possibility of being caught in a dangerous situation.

"How worried should we be?" asked James.

"We are safe here," replied Alex. "I am not sure what this is about, but they are keen to progress with the meeting. We might get some more information in it."

They followed Alex to the stairs and made their way to the meeting.

It was a 2-hour session. No mention of anything happening outside the windows was made. Several times, James tried to broach the subject but was cut off quite curtly. He was told clearly that it was nothing to be worried about.

When the meeting finished, James and Ben set off straight back to their hotel to try to make contact with Dublin to try to find out what was going on. Their bosses in Dublin, unsurprisingly, had not heard anything. They decided to send Alex out to try to get some more information.

"We will stay here in the hotel and keep an eye out – if it looks dangerous, Alex, come straight back here. We will look after you too." The hangover had long disappeared from James's head. His main priority now was making sure that both he and Ben could get themselves out of any potentially tricky situation.

"Get on to Dublin again Ben and find out when is the earliest we can fly out of here."

Ben nodded and picked up the phone.

A couple of hours later, Alex knocked on the bedroom door. He rushed in and filled his friends in on the news he had found.

"There was a press conference held in the building of the Central Committee of the Communist Party of Lithuania, and Juozas Jermalavičius, the head of the Ideological Division, announced the creation of the "National Salvation Committee of Lithuanian SSR," and that from now on it will be the only legitimate government in Lithuania. The Minister of Foreign Affairs has also sent a diplomatic note to the Ministry of Foreign Affairs of the Soviet Union in which he expresses his concerns about Soviet army violence in Lithuania. This could be it. This could be the end of it all!"

Alex was exhilarated. His beloved Lithuania was edging closer and closer to ultimate freedom from the Soviet Union. James was not so sure. He could not believe that the Soviets would just roll over – why had they seized the Defence Department earlier if they would just cede control.

"Thanks, Alex. Ben has secured a flight out of here for us late on Sunday night – you are more than welcome to come with us?"

"Thank you. But I will stay here. Also, James, there is a man downstairs in reception looking for you – he said his name is Emilis and you would know him."

James looked up and smiled.

"I'll walk you down Alex."

Emilis was sitting in the reception area of the hotel. He stood and smiled as he saw James and Alex approach.

"What a time you picked to visit us in Vilnius" he laughed. The two men shook hands. Alex made his excuses and left telling James he would see him at some point the following day.

"A little drink to clear the head?" suggested James.

Emilis agreed to a quick drink and the pair entered the bar and sat at the counter. He told James what he had been hearing from his contacts about the happenings earlier on. He did not know what had started all of this and was not sure how it would all end up.

"I am looking to keep out of trouble James. I don't want to be caught up in this and risk losing my family again."

"We are leaving on Sunday night," James told him.

"Very well, you will come back to the restaurant tomorrow night for a final meal together. We will play music and sing and give you a send-off." Smiled Emilis.

"Sounds great. I'll even convince Ben to come along too!"

The friends parted and it was only when Emilis had left that James remembered about his watch and the paintings. He ran to the door to call after Emilis, but he had already disappeared. I will bring them tomorrow night he thought to himself and went back into the bar to have another drink.

The next morning, Ben woke up not feeling well again. His stomach was not right, and he called through to James in his room to tell him he was planning to stay in bed all day and try to get rid of the illness so he could travel the following day.

"Don't go doing anything stupid though James," he warned. "Just stay in and behave!"

James laughed and wished his old friend good health. He spent the morning packing and getting his belongings together for the trip home. He also called home and spoke to his wife, Maria, filling her in on what was going on. They had a good talk. As he hung up, after telling her that he loved her, he reflected on their lives over the past 10 years. From the unadulterated joy of their marriage and the birth of their two boys to the unfathomable sadness that engulfed them over the accident. They never spoke of it aloud, but he knew Maria blamed him somewhat for the accident. She did not say anything. She did not have to. Relations between them had been strained for weeks and months afterward. Never resulting in a full-blown fight but just simmering in the background. But they had to hold themselves together for Will's sake. He was a quiet little boy, made even quieter by what had happened. James's heart would nearly break every time Will would talk to him about Tom. It was clear that he worshipped and adored his older brother and felt a little lost without him. James tried desperately hard to ensure that he felt as loved as possible. The last thing he would ever want was for Will not to feel special in the family. Tom was his eldest, his first boy. The heir! So, there was always going to be an affinity there. It was so hard to say goodbye to him. However, he loved Will just the same. He loved the fact that he was quieter, shyer, and more reserved. He loved how much Will enjoyed spending time with his mother – the special bond that had always existed between them. He hoped his son knew how much he loved him. In fact, he made a pact with himself there and then to ensure the boy would always know how special he was. They were lucky, his family, that they had each other. And especially lucky that they lived in a beautiful, free, democratic country. They needed to start appreciating it more. What happened to Tom was in the past. He would always be with them in spirit, but they now needed to move on with their lives; the three of them together.

James ate lunch alone in the hotel restaurant. As he was finishing, Alex called in to see him. He updated him on the situation. It seemed that overnight the Soviet military had successfully seized a police station in Vilnius but had been foiled in trying to seize the police academy. There were mixed reports of fighting in other parts of the country. Alex was nearly jumping up and down on the spot as he told James all the news. The excitement was flowing through him as he felt the communist era was ending. He wished James a safe trip home and promised to see him again soon. James headed upstairs and took a short nap before showering and changing his clothes. He was going to stroll across to the restaurant to have that final meal with Emilis. He called into Ben's room on the way to let him know.

"I think you are mad," Ben protested. "Just stay in and let's get home tomorrow."

"Ben, I'll be around the corner. If anything happens, I will run back here. Or you can always come and get me." James laughed.

He left the hotel and walked the short distance to the restaurant. He chuckled to himself as he recalled the circular route Ben had led them on that first night. You could not talk to Ben about maps though – he always thought he was right.

The restaurant had its lights on and looked busy. He pushed open the door and was met with a blast of warm air and a cacophony of noise. The piano was playing, the tables were full of people eating and drinking – it felt like a party.

"James!" he turned his head to see Emilis standing and waving at him. He had a table in the corner and quickly ushered James into the other chair.

"You are just in time! I was going to start without you!"

Emilis called over Jurgis, who greeted James like an old friend, and Emilis ordered for himself and his guest.

"Nice to see you again, James," smiled Jurgis as he poured some wine and left for the kitchen.

"We are celebrating James," said Emilis. "I think it's going to happen soon – they are getting ready to leave altogether."

The two friends sat back, relaxed, and enjoyed their evening. The food was delicious, and the wine flowed. Eventually, Jurgis asked Emilis to play some piano and the big man obliged without hesitation. Sitting there, listening to him on the piano, James was again struck by what a talented man he was. His large frame crouched over the piano, eyes closed, his hands gliding across the keys, producing beautiful music. Emilis stopped and called for James to join him.

"One last song from our Irish friend," he roared, and the diners all applauded. James was making his way over to the piano laughing when the door of the restaurant burst open.

A young man shouted at the crowd and silence quickly took over the room. Emilis stood, listening to the man. All over the restaurant, men stood up and grabbed their coats and belongings. Emilis looked at James.

"What happening?" James asked.

"A convoy of Soviet tanks and military vehicles is moving through the city" Emilis replied, a worried look on his face.

"Jesus!" exclaimed James, "Where are they going?"

"Looks like they are heading towards the TV Tower. This man is from the National Salvation Committee – they have tried to take power."

"Where is everyone going?" asked James as he noticed the men streaming out the front door, being called back by their wives and partners.

"They are going to the TV tower," Emilis replied quietly.

"I've got to go too, James" he said.

"Emilis. You said you would not get involved this time."

"I have to – this is my country. I am just going to see what is happening – I will stand back," he replied.

"Then I am going with you," said James putting on his coat.

"Come on, then" Emilis smiled. "I always heard you Irish were mad!"

They joined the ranks of men fleeing the restaurant and found themselves running down the street. James felt exhilarated. He knew it was partly to do with the alcohol in his bloodstream, but he was caught up in the excitement of it all. He looked at his watch to check the time but was again reminded that he did not have it on.

"Emilis, we forgot to exchange the paintings for the watch," he shouted at Emilis.

"Don't worry – we can do it tomorrow," Emilis shouted back.

"What time is it anyway?" James asked.

"It is 1 am," shouted Emilis.

It was Sunday morning. Sunday, January 13th, 1991.

Earlier on Saturday evening, Ben woke up startled by banging on his door. He got up, feeling slightly better, and answered the door. It was Alex. He pushed past Ben into the room.

"Things are getting worse. I think you and James should leave now."

"What has happened?" asked Ben.

Alex explained how a convoy of military vehicles had set off from a military base towards the city Centre. The National Salvation Committee had declared at the Supreme Council that it was their duty to take over Lithuania to avoid an economic meltdown and a war. The convoy had not stopped and in fact, another convoy was now on its way to the TV tower.

Ben rang the embassy in Germany immediately. They had been organising the change of flights for Sunday evening. He was put on hold as the envoy was found and then placed through to his private residence. Ben explained the situation.

"Stay by your phone. I will arrange something and call you back."

"Alex. I need you to go get James. He has gone to the restaurant we ate in a couple of nights ago. Do you know where that is?" Ben asked.

"I do," Alex called out as he ran out the door.

Ben started to pack quickly, hoping his friend was ok.

20 minutes later his phone rang – he answered immediately, and it was his contact in the embassy.

"There is a flight leaving Vilnius for Berlin at 06.05 this morning. I have you both booked on it."

"Thank you so much – we will make that. See you later," Ben hung up the call.

He paced the room, waiting for James to get back with Alex. He looked at his watch. It was 12.45 am.

Alex came back 20 minutes later, covered in sweat. He had run all the way back.

"James isn't there."

"Where is he, then? Did you check his room?" asked Ben.

"No. He was there alright but he left. With them all. They've gone to the TV Tower!"

"What! Fucking hell James!" exclaimed Ben.

"Right. I need a taxi now. I need to get him. Go downstairs and get the key for his room from reception. Explain to them it's an emergency".

Alex ran down, got the key, and ordered a car from the driver he had been using all week. He raced upstairs and went into James's room. Thankfully, James had packed his bags earlier so Alex grabbed them and went to Ben's room. Ben was in the process of leaving his room too.

They went downstairs and Ben checked out. Alex was outside and the car pulled up just as Ben joined him. Alex leaned into the driver and explained where they needed to go. The driver shook his head.

"He won't go to the TV tower," said Alex.

Ben reached into his pocket and took out some cash – he passed it to Alex.

"Make it happen, Alex."

Alex smiled and went back over to the driver, who seconds later jumped out and left the engine running.

"Hop in, Ben," said Alex smiling as he sat into the driver's seat. "I'll bring you myself."

They tore off with a screech of tires and set off towards the TV tower. There were throngs of people on the streets and Alex blew the horn to get them out of his way. They made it to the TV tower in 10 minutes and Ben shouted at Alex to pull in.

He jumped out of the car and scoured the crowd for James. He finally saw him, standing away from the crowd, looking out of place and scared. He ran over to them and pulled James aside by the arm.

"James, what the fuck are you doing? Get in the car. We need to leave now. This is getting too dangerous. We are going to be caught up in a firefight."

James looked towards the melee that had erupted around the TV tower. He could just about hear the rumbling of tanks as they approached. He knew Ben was right. In the distance, he could see Emilis, gesturing wildly at a group of men surrounding him. He shouted over to him, but his voice was lost in the wind.

"Ok, let's get the hell out of here."

James ran over to the car and jumped in the passenger seat. He laughed as he saw it was Alex driving.

"Alex to the rescue!" he shouted as Alex revved the engine and swung the car around. As the car turned in the road, the first Soviet tanks could be seen approaching. A roar went up from the crowd gathered at the tower. James looked out the grimy window of the cab and could see Emilis standing, fist raised in the air, screaming from the top of his lungs.

Alex drove at breakneck speed to the Airport. He screeched the car to a halt at the departure terminal. He jumped out and helped Ben and James get the bags out of the car.

Ben took another wad of notes from his pocket and stuffed them into Alex's pocket.

"Thank you, my friend. You have saved us," he said.

"My pleasure." smiled Alex, "safe trip, home. I will see you both soon."

James was quiet. He shook Alex's hand and followed Ben into the terminal.

Once there, they knew they were safe.

Ben explained to James about the flight to Berlin.

"Thanks, Ben. I'm sorry I went," James said sheepishly.

Ben laughed. "Of course, you went James. You can't help yourself."

"Thanks for coming to get me."

"You are welcome. I couldn't face Maria if I had left you behind," Ben smiled at James.

Hearing her name, James suddenly needed to ring home. He spoke to Maria to tell her the new change of plans.

"Are you safe?" She asked.

"Yes. I am safe. Give Will a kiss for me. I will be home tomorrow. I love you."

As the plane taxied down the runway and eventually took off, James looked out of the window and watched as Vilnius came into view and then disappeared again as the plane moved through the clouds. He wondered what was happening down there. And he wondered how Emilis was doing.

Chapter 10

Dublin, 1991

It was difficult to find out any information about what had actually happened in Vilnius. Newspaper reports were scarce, and James could not get a clear answer on what had taken place that night at the TV tower. He had the landline number for Emilis's apartment, but it just kept ringing out. He tried to get hold of Alex to see if he could find any information on the ground, but he was also uncontactable leaving James frustrated at the fate of his friend. Finally, after another day had passed, Alex called him back. And filled him in. They were calling it the 'January Events'. Soviet forces at the TV tower killed 13 civilians. Many more were in the hospital. The tanks ploughed through the crowd, crushing some and soldiers opened fire on the others. The names of the dead had not yet been released. Almost 100,000 people had gathered after the carnage to protest. James asked Alex to go to Emilis's apartment and check in on him. But he refused.

"It's still dangerous out there. I am going nowhere. When I can, I will. You were lucky, James – if we had arrived five minutes later you could have been killed."

Alex rang back the next day with the names of the 13 dead.

Loreta Asanavičiūtė
Virginijus Druskis
Darius Gerbutavičius
Rolandas Jankauskas
Rimantas Juknevičius
Alvydas Kanapinskas
Algimantas Petras Kavoliukas
Vidas Maciulevičius
Titas Masiulis
Alvydas Matulka
Apolinaras Juozas Povilaitis
Ignas Šimulionis
Vytautas Vaitkus

Hearing Alex read these names out as he sat in his office in Dublin, James realised just how lucky he had been. He had an odd sense of elation, as Emilis's name was not amongst them. He must have made it through he thought. He picked up his phone and once again dialled the number Emilis had given him on a scrap of paper. He had lost count of how many times he had tried it. It rang and rang. Still no answer.

Weeks passed. Slowly but surely, the international world took notice of what had happened in Lithuania. Violence had spread to more places than Vilnius. The death count grew to 15 – one more civilian, Vytautas Koncevičius, who died from his injuries in hospital, and 1 Soviet soldier, killed by a stray bullet from one of his one colleagues. Condemnation from George Bush and other strong Western reactions helped to influence the signing of a treaty between Lithuania and the Soviet Union on January 31.

On February 4, 1991, just three weeks after the attacks, Iceland publicly and formally recognised the Republic of Lithuania as a sovereign independent state, and diplomatic relations were established between the two nations. And just days after, Lithuanians turned out in force for a referendum on the full and total independence of Lithuania – a landslide victory with 90% of the vote. The dream was fast becoming a reality.

However, there was still no word of Emilis. Alex went to visit his apartment but reported back to James that there was no sign of anyone, let alone Emilis. The phone continued to ring out, unanswered.

Life and work took over again for James. Following the excitement of Vilnius, it was decided to pause travel to Eastern Europe for a couple of months until things settled down. James was desperate to get back to Lithuania – desperate to see what happened with Emilis. He scoured newspapers, travelling to the library in the City Centre weekly to look at as many international newspapers as he could to try and discover updated casualty lists from what was now being called 'Bloody Sunday'. But he found nothing relating to his friend.

Finally, in late August, nearly eight months later, a trip to Vilnius was approved. It was a 2-day trip – with meetings back-to-back on both days. James was travelling with Ivan, a junior member of staff from the office on this trip. Ben was otherwise engaged and was not too sorry not to have to travel back. James and Ivan checked into the same hotel as before. On the first evening, after a long day of meetings, James suggested they go for a walk to get some air and get something to eat. He led Ivan through the streets and back to Jurgis's restaurant. However, it was closed. Peering in through the windows, James could see it had been closed for a while. There was no sign of life at all. Starving, they went to another restaurant nearby. James was anxious and was bad company throughout the meal. His mind was elsewhere, trying to figure out what else he could do to find out what had happened to his friend. As they walked back towards the hotel, James announced that he needed more fresh air, so was going to take another walk. He would see Ivan in the morning.

He set off towards the apartment block where he had visited Emilis. It already seemed like a lifetime ago. It was a beautiful late summers evening in Vilnius and there were plenty of people out and about on the streets. He smiled as he saw groups of young people lounging on grassy areas, having a drink outside cafes, and generally enjoying life. What a change since the last time he was here.

He finally made it to the apartment block and climbed the stairs to Emilis's apartment- nothing looked different from the outside. He knocked and took a step back. He could hear no movement from inside. He knocked again. The door to the apartment beside it opened and an elderly woman peered out at James. She spoke to him in Lithuanian – but it did not take a translator to let James know that she was not welcoming to him.

"Emilis." James pointed at the apartment.

The woman shook her head.

"Lina. Audra?" He pointed again.

She shook her head again. And spoke to him. She had a sad look on her face and her eyes began to water. James felt a strange sense of doom as he tried to figure out what she was saying.

"Dead," He asked. She looked blankly at him. He made an act of cutting his throat.

The woman paused and looked at him.

"Ne," she said. No. James' heart rose. The woman made actions with her hands suggesting they had left.

"Klaipėda," she said.

"Aciu," James replied. "Thank you."

He turned to leave but the woman stepped forward and grabbed his arm. She leaned in and spoke furiously into his face, spittle hitting his cheeks. She was irate and upset about something.

James pushed her off, "I am a friend," he said.

The woman stopped and turned on her heel, slamming the door behind her.

James made his way out of the apartment block. He leaned against the wall in the late evening sun and smiled to himself. Emilis was alive and he was with his family. They must have decided to get out of Vilnius and move back to Klaipėda – to get away from the trouble. No wonder nobody was answering his calls.

He could relax now and forget about his friend. He stopped for a beer on the way back to the hotel; and before he took his first sip of the ice-cold lager, he raised his glass in a silent toast to his friend.

"Enjoy your beautiful family in your beautiful country, Emilis. I hope we meet again one day."

Chapter 11

Dublin, 2020.

Lithuania in January 1991. I knew that Dad had travelled through a lot of the Eastern Bloc in the early 1990s. And most of the time he was with Ben. Ben had come to Dad's funeral. He had stood outside, and we caught up afterwards. I had not seen him in years. He was one of Dad's closest colleagues and best friends. They travelled everywhere together. And later, when they both retired, they would meet up for long walks and even longer lunches. Reminiscing on the old times, I presume. If anyone would know whom this note was from, it would be Ben.

I searched through Dad's old notebooks and address books looking for Ben's mobile number. I finally found it and gave him a call. He was delighted to hear from me, and we arranged to have a coffee later in the week. I did not get into the details with him.

We met at a coffee shop near Ben's house. I was there first and watched him walk up the street – I was struck by how old he had become as he struggled to open the door of the coffee shop. It reminded me of how old Dad had become. In my mind, they were always two middle-aged men, travelling across Europe and the World together having the time of their lives.

After greeting each other and ordering our coffees, we sat down and exchanged pleasantries. Ben asked about my family and asked how we were all coping without Dad. I explained how difficult we were all finding it. I asked him about the old days and how they used to travel.

"Your father was the best travelling companion I could have asked for. He was so full of excitement to be seeing new places. Back then, we went places that nobody here had even of heard of. But we loved it. We preferred it better when it was just the two of us. We loved to try new foods, immerse in culture, and visit art museums. Things you wouldn't have expected from what we were in essence – two mid-level project managers!"

I asked Ben specifically about Lithuania in 1991 and if he remembers an artist, they would have come across.

"Emilis," Ben blurted straight away. "How could I forget Emilis and Vilnius in 1991?"

He began to tell me the story of how they met Emilis and all the events leading to their departure from Vilnius under the cover of darkness.

"I was sick for the last 3 days of that trip – some sort of stomach bug – so I didn't know Emilis as much as your dad. But he struck a chord with James. For weeks afterwards, he was obsessed with trying to contact him, to find out what had happened to him that night. He had me using all of my back channels in Vilnius to try to get any information – and I tried them all. But there was nothing. It was as if Emilis and his family had simply vanished. Your Dad took this hard – he felt a sense of allegiance to him I suppose as he had been with him up to the point, we saw the tanks arrive. I genuinely feared for our lives that night as we drove away in the taxi. I am not sure your dad really understood the seriousness of the situation. He loved a bit of drama, and he was caught up in the spirit of the whole thing. But when we read the reports the following day and weeks and heard how many people died, right where he was standing, it brought it home to him. He kept trying to reach them. And he kept trying to convince our bosses to send us back to Vilnius. They were slow to do so as we all wanted to see how the new independence would play out before we jumped back in. Most of the contacts we had been dealing with had remained in place – they were all Lithuanians anyway – so we were working the phones with them, making sure they still had us in mind for any large projects."

Ben took a break and I ordered us both another coffee.

"When an opportunity arose for us to send someone in later that year, August I think, James jumped at it. There was no need for the work to be carried out by someone at his level. That is why I did not go on that trip – Ivan, instead accompanied him, on his first trip incidentally, but nothing was keeping James away. I spoke to him before he left, and he was already working out ways to try to track Emilis down. Remember there had been zero contact since we had left. And there were no mobile phones back then or no email. He had a landline number, which he was not even sure was correct. And we had sent a few people around to the apartment block to knock on the door – but to no avail."

"When he returned a week later, we met up for lunch. James was elated. 'They went back to Klaipėda,' he told me. I asked him how he was sure, and he told me of a conversation he had in broken English with their neighbour. She told him

115

that they were alive and well and had left for Klaipėda. It made sense to James –that is where Lina was from and Emilis would have wanted to keep his family safe. He did not pursue it any further. He was satisfied that his friend was safe and did not want to intrude too much."

And that seemed to be the end of it.

Once he got back from that trip, I did not hear him speak of it again. Of course, that's when all the trouble with your mother started."

I paused and looked at Ben. I had not thought about the timing. September 1991. Mum got sick just before Christmas of 1991. I was 11.

Chapter 12

Meath, 1991

I can remember coming home from school on a Tuesday afternoon to find Mum and Dad sitting in the kitchen. It must have been late October. It was odd that they were both there. Dad was normally at work; he was never around during the day. I could see from Mum's face that she had been crying, but when I walked into the room, she jumped up and fussed over me, making me a sandwich, and asking me about my day. Dad remained sitting at the table, staring out the window. His cup of tea was untouched in front of him, stone cold. I wanted to ask what was wrong but could not find the words or the courage. So, I left them there, took my sandwich with me and left the room.

I stopped outside the door and listened in.

"We have to tell him," I heard Dad say.

"Not yet. It is nearly Christmas. Can we leave it for a bit?" my Mum replied.

I stood there, frozen, for a minute trying to figure out what on earth they could be talking about. I did not have the type of relationship with my parents, or the personality for that matter, to simply barge back into the room and demand to know what they were talking about.

Instead, I walked away and tried to push it to the back of my mind.

However, it did not stay in the background for long. Three weeks later Mum and Dad sat me down and explained that Mum had found a lump in her breast. It was cancer. They were quite abrupt and forthcoming with the information. I sat there saying nothing, hundreds of questions spinning around in my head. But one main one. Did this mean Mum was going to die? Mum must have sensed my feelings as she reached over and grabbed and my hands.

"It's called Cancer but it's not really." She smiled at me. "I am starting treatment next week, which is why we are telling you now. I will have to go to the hospital every week and get radiotherapy. And that will cure it. And I will be fine. And things will go back to normal."

As she spoke, I happened to glance at Dad. He was sitting ashen-faced looking out the window. Looking like somebody had punched him in the gut.

And so, we began a routine of dealing with cancer. Mum would go to the hospital every week for her treatment. Sometimes Dad would go with her, sometimes not. He was suddenly around a lot more. His travel seemed to stop, and he concentrated all his energy and attention on Mum. Mum reacted differently each time to her treatment. Some weeks she was fine, carrying on as if nothing had happened. But some weeks it would take its toll. She would be wiped out. Lying in bed for days – so alien to how she normally acted. She would never talk about how she felt though. Anytime I would ask her she would reply straight away

"I'm fine – how are things with you? How's school?"

Christmas was more reserved that year. It was just the three of us at home. No guests. Mum was tired and could not deal with hosting, so it fell on Dad and me to attempt to make Christmas dinner. He had been in the house more in the past couple of months, but I still felt that I had not spent much time with him. This project brought us together for a couple of days at least.

The Christmas dinner itself was a triumph. Dad and I spent the day in the kitchen, with Mum at the table doling out instructions. We laughed. A lot. Dad and I had become very close over the short period. We both desperately just wanted to look after Mum. And we both did not want to talk about the illness or imagine what could happen in the New Year.

The turkey was moist and delicious. I even made Angels on Horseback, Mum's favourite.

Dad came into my room as I was turning off the light later that night.

"Everything ok in here?"

"Yep. I had a great day, Dad."

"Me too. Good night. I love you."

"I love you more."

"Impossible." He smiled and turned off the light.

Life continued in the same rhythm for us after Christmas. Mum had her treatment; I had my school and Dad spent more time at home. On the days Mum was in treatment or just simply tired, he would collect me at the gates of school – something he had never done before. We would walk home, and I would hardly draw breath telling him everything that had happened to me on that particular day. He would help me with my homework, and we would make dinner together. I was experiencing that strange feeling of shame at being happy to spend so much time with Dad because of Mum's illness. He was around at the weekends too – we would head off for walks or play football in the garden. Both of us fighting over who would be Manchester United in our games.

Mum's treatment was going well and her consultant was very happy with her progress. She needed a couple more rounds of treatment and then would have a full body scan – to see if cancer had gone. Or spread. By this stage, she had embraced her hair loss and cut it short. She would wear a scarf or a hat any time she left the house, but while inside she would leave them off, proud of her hair. I got so used to it after the initial shock. She was becoming herself again, getting stronger as the weeks and months progressed.

As I neared the end of primary school, Dad picked me up one Thursday afternoon and took me for a longer walk home than normal. He told me that Mum and he had decided it would be best for me to go to boarding school to start secondary school. I was stunned. I had no idea this was in the plan. Actually, I was not sure if this was always the plan for both Tom and me. I guess I will never know. I did not react immediately, and we continued on our walk. When we arrived home, Mum was sitting in the kitchen. It was clear that they had discussed this beforehand. Mum jumped up as we came in and busied around me. She was telling me how much fun I would have and how many friends I would make. However, her eyes were telling a different story. I could see the sadness. And I was the same. I wanted to jump up and shout out "I don't want to go. I want to stay here with you. To look after you and make you happy."

But I did not. I smiled back and pretended to be enthusiastic. Inside I was heartbroken. I was sad.

Disappointed and sad. Why would they send me away? After all we had been through and were going through. I couldn't help but think was this Dad pushing me to leave? Did he just want Mum all to himself?

I finished primary school at the end of June. We had no holidays planned that year, as Mum would still have to go to her treatment. However, we took a couple of small trips, the 3 of us, around the country. I put the impending move to boarding school to the back of my mind and I had a magical, memorable summer of fun with both Mum and Dad. Mum was in great form and returning to her normal self. We had long walks on long beaches, just the 3 of us. I was so happy to have the full attention of both my parents to myself.

The summer ended quicker than I had hoped. Before I knew it, I was being measured for school uniforms and book lists were being fulfilled. I can remember the day I left for boarding school. Mum sitting in the kitchen, as usual, telling me what a great new adventure I was setting off on. However, as I set off in the car with Dad, I looked back to see her standing at the kitchen door, tears streaming down her face, waving me goodbye.

In the end, I really enjoyed boarding school. Sure, the first few weeks were tough as I got to know my new surroundings but once that had passed, I flourished. Unlike my primary school, where everyone had known about Tom, I was my own person in this school. I could do my own thing, be myself, and not have to live up to the ideal of Tom. I also did not have to tell everyone about him or the accident and so did not have to endure the sad looks from teachers or people constantly asking me was I ok. I came home most weekends, and these became more special too. I would catch up with Mum and Dad as much as I could filling them in on my new life and adventures. In the first half of term, we all got the news we were waiting for. Mum was cancer-free. We went out to a nice restaurant to celebrate. It really felt like a seminal moment for us all. Dad was in great form, helped by copious amounts of wine it must be said and tried to start a singsong in the restaurant much to Mum and mine's embarrassment. Life was good and felt like it was getting back to normal.

And life kept being normal for the next couple of years. We settled into our new lives. Me, at boarding school. Mum, back at home and now working part-time. And Dad, back at work properly too. He still was not travelling as much as he used to. I guess he had become used to being around a bit more and enjoyed it. Perhaps more than he thought. I did not come home every weekend anymore– but still at least 2 weekends a month. And the holidays were ours. Christmas, Easter, and Mid Terms at home and then three glorious months of summer would stretch out in front of me. While we would always go away for a short trip, either at home or abroad, it was the time I had at home, particularly when it was just mum and me that I remember and treasure the most. Watching Wimbledon together. Then grabbing our rackets and playing in the garden, me always wanting to be Pete Sampras. Some baking, some gardening – but most of all just hanging out. Dad was there too, intermittently, mainly at weekends. The best of times. This was the happiest I had been in my entire life.

Chapter 13

Meath, 1995

And that happiness lasted for a while. However, like everything else, it all changed. On a visit home when I was 15, I experienced an awful sense of déjà vu. I jumped off the bus at the end of our road as usual and ran down the lane to our house, bundling in through the kitchen door. Mum and Dad were sitting at the kitchen table. Quiet. I felt an awful sense of foreboding. So much so that I wanted to turn around and run out the door. To go far away from here and whatever news was making Mum cry and Dad look like he had seen a ghost. If they did not tell me, I could not hear it and it was not true. However, that is not how life works.

The Cancer was back. Mum had been having trouble eating food, even swallowing for a while, and had gone to get it checked out. Her doctor did not like what he saw and so referred her to a consultant. That was a week ago and they had been in to see the consultant earlier that day.

Oesophageal cancer. Not good.

I ran to Mum and hugged her. I felt her break down in tears on my shoulder, her whole body shaking. While I held her as she cried, I noticed how thin she had become. I had not been home in a couple of weeks but how had I not noticed her weight loss before?

As usual, I began looking for solutions. But nobody had any. At least not yet. The consultant wanted to see Mum again in a week where he would formulate a plan of treatment. Mum, after her initial reaction, was putting on a brave face as usual. Quick to point out how successful the consultant was and how they seemed to have caught it early.

"I've beaten it before, Will. I'll just have to do it again." She smiled at me.

We spent the rest of the weekend looking for ways to talk about something else. But it hung over us all the time. I had so many questions again. Dad would not answer them. He could tell I was looking for answers and he avoided being on his own with me all weekend.

By early December, he had no choice but to talk to me. One Saturday morning, Dad had to call an ambulance to bring Mum to the hospital. She had woken up coughing and literally could not stop. I stood and watched as her body wracked in pain from the seemingly never-ending cough. Dad was frantic, roaring down the phone urging them to come faster. When they did arrive, he suddenly seemed to remember that I was there, shouting at me to mind the house. Mum held on to my hand as the paramedics wheeled her into the back of the ambulance. I was numb. Not scared. Not crying. I stood at the front door and watched the ambulance speed away; I could see Dad's face peering out the back window at me.

He returned a couple of hours later and we sat in the kitchen. Dad did not hold back when talking to me. She was in a bad way. The consultant was hoping he could operate but was not sure.

"Can I see her?" I asked.

"Of course. She is okay now. She might have to stay in hospital for a while, but she will be home." He replied.

"Will she die?" I asked.

Dad looked at me for what felt like several minutes.

"I don't know," he said.

I was not expecting him to be that honest. I wanted him to tell me she would be fine. That she would be around for years yet.

It was awkward. It felt like we did not have much to say to each other after that.

Mum ended up staying in hospital for two and a half weeks. I went in to see her as much as I could. She would sit up in her bed and act like everything was fine. Every time I arrived, I would ask her how she was, and she would deflect the question each time, instead of asking me how I was getting on in school, or how my rugby training was going. She had stories about the other patients on the ward. And she had gossip on all of the doctors and student doctors who would come and see her.

"Will you be home for Christmas?" I asked her one day.

"Of course, I will be. Do not worry. This will all be sorted. I am going to have an operation after Christmas, and it will work."

She did come home for Christmas. Another strange Christmas in our family. Dad and I made every effort to make it as normal as possible. We got a tree, we got the decorations down from the attic, ending up in tears of laughter as Dad tried to climb down the ladder holding on to the boxes. There was a crash as he fell down the last couple of steps, half the decorations smashing on the floor.

Dad ordered a small turkey and we set out Mum's cookbooks on the table and tried to work out how to make a Christmas dinner for the three of us on our own.

Mum made it home on December 23. We both went to collect her. We were excited. Excited that she was coming home but also excited to see what she thought of our handiwork.

Mum was weak. Really weak. However, when we arrived back at the house, she tried her best to be upbeat. She came in from the car grabbing my arm as we walked in through the door. I was holding her arm and could feel her bones through her jumper. She had lost so much weight. Looking back, it was so obvious that something was terribly wrong before her diagnosis. Her appetite had disappeared. She was tired. All the time. She had stopped playing tennis and seemed to go for fewer walks.

I had lit the fire and brought Mum over to her chair in front of it. She settled into the chair, commenting to us both how proud she was of us and how well the place looked. Dad and I looked at each other and smiled. Dad gave me the thumbs up.

"Who is for a cup of Tea?" he asked.

"It's all I've been waiting for!" Mum replied.

We struggled our way through Christmas Day. Another Christmas of just the three of us. The food was ok. There were not many presents – all of our focus had been on Mum in the leadup. I did not mind; I was just so happy she was home.

After we had eaten, Mum moved back in front of the fire. She dozed off quickly and Dad and I sat up, playing card games and watching her.

It was as if neither of us wanted the night to end. We put log after log on the fire and kept playing 'one more game'.

Finally, when the logs had gone and neither of us could keep our eyes open, Dad picked Mum up and carried her upstairs to their bedroom. She was so frail. I stood at the door and watched him lay her down on the bed, and give her a kiss on her forehead.

I cried myself to sleep thinking of what could happen after Christmas. How would we cope without Mum? She was the rock of our little family. As I was drifting off, I could have sworn I heard Dad downstairs crying too. I crept out of bed and looked through the bannisters downstairs. The kitchen light was on, and I could hear Dad.

I went downstairs and opened the door. He was sitting at the table, a glass of whiskey in his hand, and tears streaming flowing freely down his face. I said nothing but sat beside him and put my arm around his shoulders. He leaned into me and buried his head in my shoulders.

After a moment, he sat back up.

"We are going to be okay, Will. Whatever happens, you and me – we are going to be ok. We've got each other."

"I know, Dad. I know."

But I did not. I did not know how we would cope.

In January, Mum and Dad met with the consultant who was keen to press on with an operation to try to remove the tumor that had formed. He wanted to do it as soon as possible and so scheduled it for late January. Mum had to go into hospital for a couple of days beforehand to be monitored so Dad took me out of school for the week and it was just the two of us rattling around the house. We tried not to talk about what was happening but that just left long empty silences. Dad was not a cook. However, he tried his best. We got some laughs out of the efforts both of us put forward to eat. Mum had looked after both of us so well.

We would both go in to visit Mum every morning – she was in good spirits – seemingly convinced that the operation would be a complete success. As usual, she deflected all talk of herself back onto me. And I was only too happy to find something else to talk about, to give us all a change of topic. The night before the operation, Mum was in a reflective mood – talking about how much she had enjoyed our Christmas and how she could not wait to be better next Christmas and help us out with all the cooking and decorating. We left her in good spirits. On the way home in the car, I asked Dad what the consultant had told him about the chances of success, "Honestly, he said 50-50." Dad replied.

I was not expecting that.

I could not concentrate the next day. Any task I started was left unfinished. I was making a cup of tea in the kitchen when Dad came rushing in. "She is out," he told me. "I don't know how it went but she is ok now. I am going in to see her later– I'll bring you in tomorrow."

"What did the consultant say?" I asked.

"He was really quick on the phone. I did not really get to ask him. He's going to meet us tomorrow at the hospital."

"Can I come?"

"I'm not sure. I think it might be best if I meet him just with Mum. I'll tell you everything he says after."

The next day I spent the morning pacing the house wondering what was happening. Finally, Dad came back from the hospital at about 2:00 p.m. He walked into the kitchen slowly and turned on the kettle. I could tell it was not good news.

"What's happened, Dad?"

He had his back to me, fussing about getting cups and tea bags ready. His shoulders began to shake. I realised he was crying.

"Dad! What is it? Tell me, please?"

He turned to face me, tears streaming down his face. He shook his head.

"It's too big. They couldn't get it out."

My mind could not really compute what he was saying.

"Are they going to try again? Something different."

Dad shook his head. "It's too late and too advanced. We just need to mind her now."

I hugged Dad as hard as I could. Still, no tears had formed. I was in shock. I think I understood what he was telling me. Mum was dying. There was nothing anyone could do. This horrible cancer has taken hold and was not moving. Actually, it was growing inside her. Wasting her away.

All I wanted to do was to see Mum.

"She's sleeping now; she's very tired after the operation. Let's have some lunch and we can go back in later," Dad told me.

We went in later that evening. Mum was sitting up in her bed but looked wrecked. She smiled as I walked into the room, but I could see a grimace that she quickly tried to hide. Her eyes looked tired. She looked thinner. She looked sick. She did not mention the operation once for the hour that I was there, instead of talking about everything else and still talking about next Christmas. I was fighting back tears. All I really wanted to do was hug her and tell her everything was going to be ok. Tell her how much I loved her and how I did not know how I was going to cope without her.

Mum came out of hospital 2 weeks later. I had gone back to boarding school for those 2 weeks but the day before she came home, Dad came to collect me. When I look back now, I realise that the doctors and Dad had let her come home to die. I still do not know how much she knew about all of this, but knowing my Mum, I would presume she understood it all. She had aged incredibly in 3 weeks. She was like an old woman when she came home. Everything she did seemed to sap the energy from her. She was also starting to hallucinate from the drugs she was taking. Moments when she did not know where she was or even who Dad and I was. One morning Dad went off to the shops and I was alone with Mum in the house. She was sitting in her chair at the window, with the sun shining on her. She suddenly turned to me and asked me to let Tom in the door.

"There's no one there, mum," I said.

She looked at me quizzically. "Just open the door and let him in and stop messing," she said.

I was scared. I went to the door and opened it to show her. There was nobody there.

"Look, Mum, no one there."

She looked at me but it felt like she was looking through me. It was an awful feeling. I wanted Dad to come back. I went over to Mum, held her hand, and rubbed it gently. She closed her eyes and went to sleep. I sat there for a while looking at her. Thinking of all the amazing times we had had together. My Mum. Whom I loved more than anything else in the world. Dad came back and found me there. He quietly put the shopping bags down and came and sat beside us. No one said anything. We all sat in silence for another while, happy together.

She lasted 3 weeks at home with us. It was tough, and harrowing and emotional and trying. However, I would not change it now for the world. After 3 weeks, she was so weak that we had to bring her into the hospital. She was induced into a coma, and she went into intensive care. We thought she would come out of it. She never did. They turned off her life support 5 days later. Dad and I were in the room alone with Mum and a palliative care nurse. Dad wanted it that way – his family and Mum's brothers and sister tried to come in, but Dad just wanted it to be the three of us. We talked to her, told her stories, and told her how much we loved her. Dad told her what we thought would happen to me in the future. We laughed at that. We told her that Tom would be waiting for her, that he would look after her. We kissed her head, brushed her hair, and hugged her as her heart rate began to drop. Then finally, it ended. The machine beeped. The nurse told us she had gone. In my mind, she had gone before then anyway. I had a memory etched there of Mum, healthy and smiling. That is what I wanted to keep. Not this memory of machines and tubes and a cancer-ravaged body.

The next few days were a blur. Family everywhere fussing over Dad and me. And the two of us just wanting to be by ourselves. I can remember we escaped and went for a long walk on the beach. We did not talk much but walked side by side. Dad looked different. His smile was not as fast to come to his face anymore. I was worried about him. I was worried about how he and I would get on now with just the two of us together.

Before the funeral, Dad asked me if I would write a eulogy for Mum. I was thrilled.

"Of course, I will," and I ran up to my room to start work on it. However, as the time came closer, the reality of having to stand up in front of a full church started to freak me out. Dad could see I was getting anxious.

"You are doing this for mum." He said, "Just close your eyes and imagine she is in the back of the Church listening. What would you want her to hear you talk about? What would you like her to know that you loved or will miss about her the most?"

On the day of the funeral, we went to the funeral home to see her one last time. She looked peaceful lying there, in an outfit Dad had chosen. We held hands looking at her, both of us trying not to break down in tears.

"Ok. Enough now, let's go get this done." Dad said and we headed for the Church. There was a big crowd. It was not a huge church, but it was full. I could not focus on anyone as we made our way in. One thing that struck me was the silence. Everybody was standing in pure and utter silence looking at us as we got out of the car and made our way into the church, carrying Mum on our shoulders. It was eerie.

I was nervous about my eulogy – the rest of the service passed so quickly and before I knew it, it was my turn. I stood up and smiled at Dad who gave me a wink. I made my way slowly to the lectern and laid out my notes, stealing a glance at the congregation. I could see friends and parents of friends and neighbours. And friends of Mum and Dad. And cousins and Aunts and Uncles. All looking at me. I could see some of Dad's work friends too – Ben gave me a nod and a smile. I remembered what Dad had told me and I searched for a spot down the back of the church. And I imagined I could see Mum. Sitting there, looking like the Mum I loved. Healthy and smiling at me. Looking proud of me. I smiled at her and began. I talked about all that she had done for me. Not just the big obvious things, but also all the small things she did. About how close we were. About how she came to all my matches, whatever the weather. About how much I loved her and how much I will miss her. I talked about how much fun we had all had as a family, me, Mum, Dad and Tom. And how Dad and I hoped Tom and her would now look after each other – as Dad and I would look after each other here. I did not cry. I felt happy getting the opportunity to talk about her. As I finished up, I looked back down to the back of the Church. However, of course, she was not there. It felt like a proper goodbye.

Dad hugged me as I sat back down to the applause of the Church. I felt proud that I had not let Mum down.

Three days after the funeral, Dad and I finally found ourselves on our own. Aunts and neighbours had left us, and it was just the two of us, sitting in the kitchen.

"Ok. I guess we need to figure out what normal is now." Dad said. "It's just you and me now buddy. A team."

We decided I would take another week off school. Then I would go back, and we would try to get back to some level of routine.

"No pressure though Will. This is all new. If you feel bad or sad, that is ok. Let me know. We will work through this together."

That night I was trying to get to sleep but I could not stop thinking about Mum. I finally succumbed and I had body shaking, hard to breathe, tears. I pushed my face deep into my pillow to try and not make noise or wake Dad. I did not want him to see me like this. He had lost his wife. He knew her longer than me. I needed to look after him now to make sure he was Ok.

A week later, I left and went back to boarding school. I decided to come home every weekend. I would long for the school week to be finished so I could get back to see how Dad was doing.

Every night, when I went to bed, I would cry myself to sleep.

Then one night, I did not. And I felt bad. Why had I stopped crying? Was I forgetting Mum already?

Dad took a couple of weeks off work to get things sorted around the house. Once he returned, he decided he would not travel for a while. He decided he could do his work from his home office for a year and then he would re-evaluate. It meant that he was at home all the time. Every weekend when I got the bus home from school, he would be there waiting for me. We spent all our free time together. We became so close. It was like finding a new friend. I went off to France for the last term of school. I did not want to leave Dad, but he made me go. As the summer holidays began, we began to play golf during the week, a quick nine holes here and there. We taught each other how to cook, properly. We celebrated my 16th birthday with a meal out and a trip to the pub. We lived. We survived. And we formed an unbreakable bond. We spoke about Mum all the time. Every time we would do something new or have a kitchen disaster, we would laugh at how Mum would have reacted.

Soon we were celebrating Christmas again. We stayed in our house and Dad's brother Joe and his family came to us. We all cooked together, and it was perfect. It was so much better than the previous Christmas. We had both been scared if Christmas would ever be the same again following the trauma of the previous year with Mum. But it could. And it would.

Another milestone passed when we celebrated Mum's 1 year anniversary. We got dressed up and went out for a nice meal. We told stories about Mum and laughed. And even cried a little. I think we both knew we were going to be ok. We had survived the first year – if we could do that, surely, we could survive anything. And she was always there. Always in our minds. Dad was sure to always talk about her and make sure I did not forget anything. He would tell me constantly how proud she was of me and how proud she would have been of me. Pictures of her appeared all over the house, beside pictures of Tom.

I asked him once if he thought he would ever find someone else.

"I don't want or need anyone else. She was everything to me and we lived a lifetime in our short time together. All I want now is the memories I have of her." he replied.

Around this time, Dad began to travel a small bit for work again. A couple of days at a time. I could see it reenergised him. It began to come closer to me finishing school and decisions needed to be made about college. The question of me moving to Dublin for college arose. Would I live up there or try to commute? Dad was pushing me to live in Dublin and experience it all, but I was unsure. It felt like breaking up our little bubble. I was just 18 when I received my results. I had secured a place at Dublin City University studying journalism. I was delighted and Dad took me to the pub for a couple of pints to celebrate. I loved going to the pub with Dad.

I loved watching him with a pint of Guinness. He would look adoringly at it, refusing to even touch it until it was properly settled. Then he would lick his lips, close his eyes and take a huge first gulp. Nearly getting into the pint glass. He would smack his lips together as he put the glass down. And smile.

We talked about my options.

"I think you should go. I will miss you of course, but you are only up the road. You can come home whenever you want. You can't hang out with me forever you know." He laughed.

"But I don't want to leave you on your own".

"I love that you say that. But you have to have your own life. I have had a great life. I met your Mum, I married the woman of my dreams and we had Tom and then we had you – I have got to live so much. You need to have your own experiences, make your own mistakes. You know how much I love you. These last couple of years have been bittersweet for me – I have got to spend so much time with you – time I would probably have not spent with you. That will never change. But you need to live your own life now. I will always be here whenever you need me."

It felt like the end of an era. And it felt like another bit of Mum was being chipped away. I promised her I would look after Dad. It did not feel right leaving him. Nevertheless, I did. I moved to Dublin that autumn. Mum had specifically left me some money, so Dad and I went to buy me a car. A beautiful fourth-hand Volkswagen Golf. I was so proud of it. I also found an apartment with some friends and started working in a nearby pub. Running wild and having the time of my life. In first year, I went home most weekends and hung out with Dad but as I got older, my visits home became less frequent. We talked all the time, but our relationship was changing again. I would get terrible guilt sometimes about Dad being on his own. However, my friends would convince me that this was simply the way life is. I could not spend my life worrying and minding Dad. I had to live my own life too. I guess they were right.

Time passed and before I knew it, I was in my final year in college. My visits home had become less and less frequent. Little did I know that they would soon cease all together.

Chapter 14

Meath, 2001

We had been sniping at each other all day. I had arrived down for a visit on Friday evening, we had gone out for a meal and a few drinks and Dad had started on at me about college again. He felt I could be doing better, studying more. The usual. I did not bite. I held my tongue. The next morning, we went out for a game of golf and the animosity was still there. To be honest that was nothing new for us but usually once we had played a few holes and had a few laughs, it would disappear. Not this time though. We were both very quiet for the round. There was tension. I can remember holing a chip on the Par 3 12th – and turning around to Dad with my arms raised, smiling. But he had turned his back and walked away. Something was up. I could not put my finger on it.

After golf, we went straight home. No pint in the clubhouse. I went into the kitchen and grabbed a beer. Dad did not join me. I could hear him stomping around upstairs.

Later as we sat down for a meal we had prepared in near silence, just the 2 of us at the island in Dad's kitchen, I went to the fridge for another beer. Dad made a comment about my drinking. I launched into him.

"And where have I learned that from Dad? You are one to talk."

"How dare you?" he began.

"No. How dare you? I am 21 years of age. I can have a drink whenever I feel like it. And right now, I feel like having a drink."

"Your mother wouldn't like to see you drinking this much," he came back at me.

"Don't talk about Mum. Maybe if Mum were here, I would not be drinking. But she is not. She's gone."

"Oh, I know she's gone. I know that every day when I wake up without her."

"I miss her too, Dad."

"Not as much as me," he snapped back.

"It's not a fucking competition, Dad, for Christ sakes."

We sat in silence for a few minutes eating. I could feel a rage building up inside of me and I was not sure what it was for. Looking at him sitting there, stubbornly chewing his food and not talking to me.

"Do I disappoint you, Dad?" I asked.

"What?" he looked up at me.

"You act like I disappoint you. I feel nothing I do will ever be good enough for you."

"Ah, shut up will you. That's nonsense and you know it."

"Well, it's how I feel. Do you think the wrong son died that day, Dad?"

"Jesus Christ!" Dad jumped up and stood over the counter looking out the window.

"Why would you bring that up now?" he said looking back at me, his eyes glistening with tears.

"I just wondered. I feel like I'm battling against Tom and I'm never going to win."

"Stop being a fool, Will. Tom is dead – dead for 15 years. I have no idea how he would have turned out – because he did not get that chance. But you did. And you are making a balls of it."

"I'm doing my best, Dad." I said looking down.

"Well, I don't think that's good enough. He protected you. He saved your life. You need to do enough for both of you. To live your life with him beside you"

"I can't do that. And he did not fucking save my life. The impact of the car knocked him over me. He was not some fucking superhero, Dad. He was nine. A little boy. And he was killed in a car crash. That's it."

"He saved you, Will," Dad shouted.

"Bullshit. And why did the car hit us, Dad?" I stood up and looked at him.

Dad stopped in his tracks. He stared at me with blazing eyes.

"No answer, eh? It hit us because you went through a red light, didn't you?"

"How fucking dare you?" In two strides, Dad was across the kitchen and before I knew what was happening, he had hit me. A right hand catching me plum on my chin. I fell back, my arms flailing at my stool but missing. I hit the ground hard, the back of my head hitting off the edge of the fireplace. I lay there, dazed for a couple of seconds. I put my hand to the back of my head and felt a warm liquid; blood. Dad was still standing over me. Frozen.

I slowly started to get up. He bent down to help me.

"Get the fuck away from me," I snarled at him.

"Will, I'm sorry. Come on get up slowly".

"Get the fuck away from me," I said again and pushed him away.

I gingerly got up and leaned against the island, feeling a steady flow of blood now running down my neck.

I went over to the sink and ran the tap, taking a tea towel off the counter as I passed. I soaked it through and held it to the back of my head. It quickly turned crimson.

"Let me have a look at that," Dad was behind me.

"I swear to God, Dad, if you come near me again, I'll fucking kill you. Get the fuck away from me."

I was trying to remember how many drinks I had had. Could I drive into town to the hospital or even just drive home? I lost count at six. I guess I was stuck here for the night.

The next morning, I woke with a pain in my head. And not just from the alcohol. I lay in bed and tried to figure out what had happened the previous day. How had it escalated so quickly? I could hear Dad downstairs. I jumped out of bed and instantly regretted that. I had to sit on the side of the bed for a minute so the pain in my head would pass. I looked down at my pillow. Nice bit of blood there. I quickly packed my bag, threw on some clothes, and headed downstairs. I did not want to talk to him, did not want another confrontation. I just wanted to get the hell out of there.

Dad was standing in the kitchen at the island drinking a mug of coffee.

"Will. How are you?" he started.

"Not now, Dad. I am going home. I'll talk to you later."

"I'm so sorry, Will."

I looked back at him. He looked sad, standing there on his own. Fuck him, I thought, turned, and walked out the door.

And that was that. I stopped into a clinic on the way home – no stitches required, just a bad cut. They tidied me up and sent me on my way. I did not call Dad that night. He tried calling me 3 times. I did not call him the next day either. Or the next. He kept trying for a week and then he stopped calling too.

My life continued. Working in a bar, drinking a lot in the same bar after hours and struggling through my final year in college. I had no idea what I was going to do with the rest of my life. I felt alone. More alone than ever before. Tom was gone. Mum was gone. Now dad was gone in my eyes too. How could he have hit me? I was all he had left.

I thought about our fight a lot. I thought about what I had said to Dad about Tom. Did I mean it? The more I thought about it, the more I believed I did. This underlying feeling of competition I had felt for all my life was coming to the surface. It was simply not fair to be constantly compared to a 9-year-old boy. Not only that, but a 9-year-old 'hero' who everybody thought had given his life for mine. I cannot remember what happened in that car. But I do not think Tom was a hero. I think he was unlucky that he was on the side of the car that directly felt the impact. The force of the other car hitting ours slammed his small body. His seatbelt took a lot of the impact, but his body was thrown sideways and landed on top of me. I loved my brother. Scrap that, I love my brother. And I always will. But I do not need the pressure of feeling as if he saved my life all the time.

I met a friend of mine, Simon, for a pint in late spring. He had decided he was going to go to Australia as soon as college was finished. For a year. Travelling around in the sunshine. Sounded perfect. I was in. All I needed was the money to get there. If I sold my car and worked full time for a couple of months, I reckoned I could afford it by September, October at the latest.

I sat my final exams, somehow scraped through them, and then worked all the hours I could for the summer. I rang Dad once, in August, after a couple of drinks and told him my plan. He kept apologising to me and wanted to come and meet me. I said no. I placated him and told him I would come down and see him before I left. I did not mean it.

I booked my flights and sold my car. I rang Dad and told him I was leaving in a week. Told him I would not be down to see him after all. Told him I was going for a year, that I needed the space, needed the time away from him after what he had done. There was silence on the other end of the line.

"I love you, Will. I am so sorry. I think it is a good thing you are going away though. I will be here when you get back," he finally spoke.

I choked up. I said goodbye and hung up quickly. When I checked my bank account later that day, I saw that Dad had made a large deposit for me.

3 days later, I was on a ferry in Brisbane, getting sunburnt.

Chapter 15

Australia.

My time in Australia can be divided into 2 parts. The first part involved me working in an Irish bar in Brisbane and a whole lot of drinking. I woke, worked, drank, slept, and repeated. Every day for about the first 6 months. I was having the time of my life if I am honest about it. I loved Brisbane. The size of the city and the people reminded me of home. And the weather just topped it all off. Everything was outside. Simon and I moved into an apartment after living in a hostel for a month. The apartment was awful, but it was perfect for the two of us. It was very close to Ballymore stadium in Brisbane, the home of the Queensland Reds Rugby Union team, so we got to experience Super 12 rugby first hand when we could manage to make it to games. We quickly settled into life in Brisbane – both working at the bar and socializing with the same crew, all from the pub. That crew was always changing. So many students and so many Irish people were on working holiday visas in Australia at the time. They would move around the country, stopping in in different locations to work for a couple of months and then move on to the next. Not us though – we stayed put in Brisbane.

After 6 months, a new girl started working in the bar. Her name was Charlotte, and she was Australian. She was beautiful. I am pretty sure that Charlotte hated me for the first couple of weeks that she knew me. I was loud, I was brash, and I was mostly drunk or thinking about being drunk. But even in my state, I could see something in her that I wanted to get to know better. So, I tried to change. I stopped drinking as much. I constantly asked her out. She constantly said no. It became a running joke in work.

"Any luck today, Will?" My co-workers would ask at the end of our shift.

"Not yet," was my reply. Every single day.

Finally, after 2 months of being asked, she relented and agreed to go out for a meal with me. Maybe it was sympathy. I'm not sure.

But whatever it was, we hit it off. I am sure Charlotte was stunned because even I was shocked at how well we got on with each other. We sat talking for hours, long after our meal was finished. I ended up telling her all about my family and Dad on that first date. I had told no one else in Australia about it. However, she just had that effect on me. I felt I could tell her anything and she would help me. She did not judge me. She did not even judge Dad. She simply asked when I was going to talk to him next.

"He's the only one left in your family, Will. He won't be around forever – will it be worth it when he's gone?"

Those words stung. I rang Dad the next morning – evening time for him. I rang the house phone. He picked up and I lost my nerve slightly.

"Hello," he gruffly called out.

"Dad, it's me." I said after a couple of seconds hesitation.

"Will!" he genuinely seemed happy.

"How are you getting on? Where are you? It's so good to hear from you."

We ended up talking for an hour. We never mentioned the incident. We talked about Brisbane, about how I was getting on. He told me how he was doing. How he was playing a bit of golf. Life was progressing. As we reached the end of the call, he asked me for my address. He said he wanted to write to me – it seemed a better way of communicating then trying to organise times for phone calls.

Dad was a brilliant writer. Particularly of letters. He would talk about the most urbane topics and have me laughing out loud as I read them. He began to send me letters every month. It reminded me of my time in France. He spoke of everyday life. The freedom he had gained from me moving away meant that he could get back to traveling with work. Not as much as before but still several times a year. He would have amazing stories from far-flung places; he began to spend a good bit of time in Africa and had some rip-roaring adventures. His conversational way of writing meant you felt like you were sitting beside him, having a pint and listening to these stories.

At the end of his first letter, he finally referred to our fight.

I cannot believe I hit you, Will. I am so ashamed. I replay the moment in my mind on a daily basis, wishing I could stop it. But I am even more ashamed that you think I loved Tom more than you. When you were born, I discovered that when you have more than one child, it is not a question of loving one more than the other. You love them equally and differently. You love them for who they are. To lose a child,

146

any child, Will, I think it is the hardest thing you can go through. I know I did not focus on you enough – I know I probably did not pay enough attention to your Mum. I could travel – get away from it all. Not deal with the pain and being around the house all the time and seeing reminders of Tom everywhere. He was my first-born son, Will. I did not ever think about having children or how it would affect me until I held him for the first time. His little fingers and toes. But I felt the same elation, astonishment, and joy when you were born too. I feel angry. Angry that he was taken away from me. Angry that he was taken away from you. And yes, angry that I was driving that night. Angry that we had a crash. Angry that the other fucker had been drinking. It changed our lives forever. That single moment. Changed who we might have been as a family. I am so sorry I could not have dealt with it better. And I am so sorry that you feel as if I loved Tom more than you. But I did not. He was a great big brother and would have always looked after you. You are my boys. I am just sorry I did not show it enough. And I hope it is not too late. You are all that I have left of my beautiful family, and I do not want to lose you too. Enjoy yourself in Australia. Live your life. Be safe. But please come back to me one day. I need you.

I sobbed as I read that piece over and over. I felt exactly the same way. I felt my life was changed forever the moment Tom was killed. The moment that car hit. I could not forgive Dad just yet. However, I did not hate him as much as I had when I left home. I would keep in touch with him.

From his letters I gathered that he had begun to go on holidays by himself too. He hated the idea of package holidays or cruises so he would take himself off to five-star hotels all over Europe for a week and stay by himself. He would send me letters from the places describing the people he saw, the things he did. And I loved them. There was always a slight tinge of loneliness that I would spot in these accounts – but that would quickly be replaced by an outrageous comment on a couple he had seen or one of the staff in hotel! Dad wrote far more letters to me than I replied. But the letters gave our relationship a pulse, albeit a slight one. There was no major reconciliation. For now, just reading his thoughts and putting, some of mine on paper was enough. Life was moving on. Again.

So began the second part of my life in Australia. The Charlotte years. Charlotte and I were inseparable. I was meant to be moving on from Brisbane in June. Simon and I had a plan to go to Sydney and then on to Melbourne. We were due to leave on the 17th of June. I know this date because Ireland played Spain in the Second Round of the 2002 World Cup the night before. The 2002 World Cup was in Japan and South Korea – which meant perfect times for watching matches for those of us in Australia. Unlike those back home who were up at all hours. I do not know what other countries involved in that World Cup remember from the tournament. But being Irish, there is only one thing. Roy Keane and Saipan. Roy, our best player, left the tournament from the island of Saipan the week before it started. He had a major row with Mick McCarthy, the Irish manager, over training facilities and walked out. The country was divided – you were either with Roy or with Mick. I was with Roy. Of course, I was, he was a Manchester United player. Dad was pro Roy too. There was an interview published in The Irish Times, which turned out to be the final straw for McCarthy. Dad sent the article in the post to me straight away. He followed up with a phone call describing it in detail and capturing the mood back home. Sitting there in my dingy apartment thousands of miles away, I felt like I was beside him as Dad lambasted McCarthy and the Football Association of Ireland.

It was a strange feeling as the World Cup began. I obviously still wanted Ireland to do well, but there was a bit of me angry that Roy was not there. The team started well with a 1-1 draw with Cameroon. Then came the Germans. Somehow, we made it to half time only 1-0 down. Then in the second half, we improved. But could not make a breakthrough. Until the last minute and Robbie Keane picked up a Niall Quinn knock down and rifled the ball past Oliver Kahn. Cue madness. I was working that night and the noise and the atmosphere in the pub was incredible.

Our final group game was a 3-0 win against Saudi Arabia – I remember it for Damien Duffs celebration alone – and we were on to the Second Round. Even without Roy.

In the week leading up to the match, I was in a bad mood. I did not want to leave Charlotte behind but could not find the courage to ask her to come with us. I had secured a night off to watch the game. Charlotte had too. We went to the pub to celebrate our last night together. The match was unbelievable. From being 1-0 down early on, Ireland battled back, and Robbie Keane scored a penalty with nearly the last kick of the game to send it to extra time. I thought the pub was going to explode as the ball hit the back of the net. I grabbed Charlotte and we hugged. I was so happy.

"Stay," she said.

"What?" I shouted back. I could hardly hear her with the noise all around me.

"Stay here. In Brisbane. With me."

The rest of the pub seemed to melt away in my mind. All I could see was Charlotte smiling at me.

"Ok!" I shouted.

The rest of the game is a bit of a blur to me. I know we dominated, and we should have won. The game went to penalties. Robbie Keane scored again. Then Matt Holland and David Connolly both missed and it looked like it was all over. Spain missing kept us alive but a further, miss from Kevin Kilbane allowed Gaizka Mendiata to score a woeful penalty to give Spain the victory. The pub was shell-shocked. We had it in our grasp – a quarter final spot and a victory over Spain. All without Roy. At the time, I could not have cared less. I was so happy.

Simon left the next morning, not as mad with me as I had expected. He told me he was dreading travelling with me anyway as I would have been acting like a lost puppy without Charlotte. Harsh but probably fair.

I had nowhere to live as we had given up on our apartment but I managed to convince the landlord to let me stay on – and Charlotte moved in with me. We were elated.

Charlotte was from Byron Bay and her family still lived there, on a winery. Byron Bay is about a 2-hour drive from Brisbane. She brought me home to meet her family about 3 weeks after Simon left for Sydney. We spent the weekend on the winery, and it was bliss. Charlotte has three sisters – all of whom still lived at home. One older who worked with her parents and two younger girls. They welcomed me warmly into their family. I enjoyed watching the sisters interact with each other – bounce off each other. It gave me a glimpse of a busy family life, full of fun. Reminded me of what I did not have. Charlotte's father, Cameron, was a quiet man obsessed with his winery, his land, and his family. On the first day, he took me for a walk for miles, all around the estate, describing each piece to me in detail and sussing out this young man his beloved daughter had brought home. As we walked, my observations on life in Australia and specifically Brisbane as an outsider had him in tears of laughter.

"Will, that's great stuff mate. You should write these down."

So, I did.

Charlotte and I moved into a new apartment in Brisbane not long after. She could not take living in our hovel anymore. My working visa was due to expire in October, so we needed to figure out what I was going to do. Would I go home or try to stay longer? I had nothing to rush home for, but I needed to get a work sponsor to keep me in Australia. I spoke to my boss at the pub to see if this was an option. He was happy to try but in order to do so he would need to make me a manager – and I would need to commit to at least 3 years working for him. I agreed on the spot. He took care of the paperwork and before I knew it, I had landed myself a promotion and I was staying put.

We spent a good bit of time in Byron Bay over the next couple of years. Charlotte was definitely a home bird and would go back home at every opportunity she could find. And I would go along too. I developed a good relationship with her family and her parents. Her father was sports mad – which gave us some common ground. We only ever had one falling out – we were watching the First Test of the British & Irish Lions tour against New Zealand in 2005. Sir Clive Woodward was the coach and Brian O'Driscoll, the Irish captain, was the touring captain. There had been a lot of comment, particularly down under, about Woodward's selection policy and the huge amount of entourage this Lions tour seemed to have. The feeling was that it was losing the magic of the previous Lions tours. A loss to the New Zealand Maoris on the 3rd match of the tour only added to the pressure on the Lions for the first test. Although a proud Australian, and so reluctant to support the All Blacks, Cameron was torn. He despised Woodward. We watched the game at his house, with a couple of beers. After 2 minutes, O'Driscoll was injured at a ruck. Replays showed Kevin Mealamu and the AllBlack captain Tana Umaga clearly spear tackling him into the ground, dislocating his shoulder in the process, and ending his tour. I say clearly but Cameron could not see the issue. He felt it was a clean clear out. My mood deepened as the All Blacks went on to win the match 21-3. The argument between Cameron and me over the tackle lasted long into the night. So much so that Charlotte and her mother, Anna, decided that we should not be allowed to watch rugby matches together again. I was so close to calling Dad that night to find out the reaction back home. I wondered if he had even seen it. Did he get up to watch it? I knew he would have agreed with me. I withheld the urge though.

I kept writing on the side. Putting everything in a book, which I always carried around with me. When I felt I had enough, I decided to look at getting something published.

Charlotte was all for it and encouraged me to approach the Courier Mail – the biggest paper in Brisbane. I had nothing to lose.

I met with an editor called Max Bradley. We talked for an hour over a coffee, and he agreed to try it out. I would get a small column on the next 2 weekend lifestyle pages and see how it went. And it went well. The reaction was good and so I was kept on. Just as an on the side sort of thing. I would submit a piece of about 700-800 words each week on musings I had about living as an Irishman in Brisbane. I loved it.

And that was how my life carried on. Weeks turned into months and months into years. We were so happy. The pessimist in me was sure it would all come tumbling down at some point soon, so I was determined to enjoy it while it lasted.

Dad continued to write to me. I continued to answer at a slower pace. I did not make any trips back to Ireland. While he did mention a couple of times that he would love to travel over to Australia, I never pursued it and neither did he. We coexisted, from afar.

Chapter 16

In the end, I spent 6 years in Australia. 4 years in Brisbane and a further two in Sydney. I somehow managed to be headhunted by the Sydney Morning Herald and Charlotte and I packed up and moved to Sydney. By that stage, I had stopped working in the pub and was concentrating on my writing full time. I had a vague idea about writing a novel – actually, in my head a series of novels. But nothing on paper yet. My life was good.

Then suddenly one day I was walking into the office in Sydney, and I had an urge to go home. I dismissed it straight away. What did I have to go home for after all? However, the feeling kept coming back. I talked to Charlotte about it. She was a bit taken aback at first. I had never mentioned going home before. But something had changed. I missed home. I could not put my finger on exactly what it was that I missed. It was not Dad specifically; it was not anyone specifically. I just missed being in Ireland. The more Charlotte and I talked about it, the more it appealed to both of us. Charlotte had never travelled before. And she desperately wanted to see Ireland. So, we made our minds up. I was going home. We were going home.

Four months later, we arrived back in Dublin. We had no jobs and nowhere permanent to live. Another adventure.

I was anxious about seeing Dad. I could not believe it had been six and a half years since I had last seen him.

I decided to go and meet him by myself first. I did not think it was fair on Charlotte for her to meet my dad at the same time as our big reunion. Or a rematch perhaps.

I rang him the day we arrived back to make plans. He was in high spirits.

"I presume you are still in the house Dad?" I asked.

"Of Course, I am. Sure where else would I be. I will see you tomorrow. I can't wait" he rang off.

I rented a car and drove down to see him the next morning. So many memories spinning through my mind as I made the familiar trip. The closer I got, the more nervous I became. I parked the car outside the house and took a deep breath. As I climbed out of the car, the kitchen door burst open, and Dad came running out. He was crying. He ran over to me and threw his arms around me.

"Will. I am so happy you are here."

I was taken aback. I was not expecting such emotion. I hugged him back.

"Come on inside."

As we walked in, I took a look at him. He looked older but was still the same Dad. Perhaps slightly smaller, with a bit less hair. Still the same wide smile. The kitchen smelled of baking.

"I made some bread," he said nonchalantly.

"You what?" I laughed aloud. "When did you turn into a baker?"

"Ha! Impressed?" He laughed.

"Definitely, Dad."

"So where is this Charlotte? When do I get to meet her?"

"All in good time, Dad" I relied.

We sat the kitchen table and looked at each other.

"7 years, Will! You look well." Dad said.

"You look well yourself." He smiled.

"I've tried to keep myself going. Getting a bit slower but still able to look after myself. I can't believe you are finally back".

We sat at that table for hours. Chatting. Sitting in silence. Getting to know each other again. We did not talk about the past. We did not have to. That was gone now. Nothing to be gained from rehashing any of that.

I left as the sun was going down. We hugged again by the car.

"I really am so happy you are here," he said, tears glistening in his eyes.

"Me too, Dad. I'll bring Charlotte to meet you next weekend."

"I would love that."

With that, I jumped in the car and drove off. As I left the driveway, I looked in my rearview mirror and could see him standing there, all alone, waving goodbye.

From the moment Dad set eyes on Charlotte the next weekend, I knew he was mad about her. They talked and laughed for hours – leaving me to sit back and watch for most of the weekend. Dad loved an audience and was the perfect host. He loved meeting new people and he was at his most charming best. He cooked up a storm as Charlotte showered him with compliments. He was as proud as punch – like a teenage boy getting praise. We went for long walks on the beach and drank nice wine in front of a roaring fire. It was perfect. It made me start to really think about Charlotte – and about spending the rest of my life with her. Seeing her in my home, with my dad, she fitted in perfectly. I missed my Mum – I really would have liked her to be there. To see what I had become. Actually, to see what Dad and I had become. The man cooked us a roast dinner for God's sake! I do not ever even remember him boiling an egg when Mum was alive. She would have been proud of us.

I do not think it was much of a surprise to anybody when I proposed to Charlotte the following year. I had called her father the previous day and asked his permission. He kept me waiting in utter silence for about 20 seconds before laughing out loud.

"Of course Will. Go for it. I think you will get the right answer."

He was still laughing at this joke as we ended the call.

Dad was away on one of his holidays in Lanzarote at the time. I rang him to tell him, and he swore profusely down the phone – much to the enjoyment of the fellow guests at the resort. He was delighted.

"I fucking knew it," he exclaimed. "About bloody time too!"

We got married 17 months later in a beautiful country house, just down the road from my family home. It was a glorious day. Late autumn but the sun came out and we could have the drinks reception outside. Dad was in his element. Cameron and himself got on like 2 long lost friends. We referenced Mum in all the speeches – but it was not with sadness. More with joy – joy that she would be happy to see us all so happy.

Dad jumped up on stage with band during the reception and sang a song. "Mr. Bojangles". The crowd lapped it up. Born entertainer. I was so happy.

There is one picture from our wedding day that I treasure. It is from the Church. It is of Dad in the foreground and behind him, you can see a couple of rows of the congregation. They are all talking to each other and animated. But Dad is still. He is looking towards the top of the Church – presumably at me. I do not think Charlotte had arrived yet. His eyes are moist. When I show it to Charlotte, she says she thinks he looks happy. However, when I look at it, I see sadness. I can imagine him looking at me and thinking about Mum and Tom. Missing them. Wishing Mum was by his side. Looking at all the other couples around him. Imagining Tom at the top of the Church beside me, more than likely my Best Man. I love that picture. It sums Dad up for me. Externally strong but internally still grieving. Unselfish. And knowing that he would be onstage singing at the top of his lungs a couple of hours after it was taken makes it even better.

Dad was 75 the following year. He was still strong but starting to slow down slightly. Mowing the lawns was taking a little bit longer. And his tee shots on the golf course were getting shorter. Our first daughter, Becky, was born and followed 2 years later by Matthew. Dad adored and was adored by them. Visits to his house were less frequent simply due to the logistics involved in transporting our growing family but when we there it was magical. He would read the children stories, play with them outside, bring down my old train sets and set them up for them all over the kitchen floor.

They made him look younger – it was as if they gave him a new lease of life.

My new family, Charlotte, Becky, and Matthew created a new stage in myself and Dad's relationship. It made us forget about the past; instead, we focused on the present. And we became closer and closer.

I was so happy to be a dad. I still am. When Becky was two, Charlotte started to talk about having another baby. I could not understand how I could love another little person as much as I loved Becky. I was scared. Scared that this is what happened to Dad – maybe he gave too much of his love to Tom.

But I was wrong. I know that now. Wrong about it all. When I held Matthew for the first time, I understood. I loved that boy with all my heart. And yet I did not love Becky any less. You love them unconditionally. And differently. Maybe your heart grows, I do not know, but there is plenty of room for two. And I am sure if you have three, four or five, it is the same.

Sometimes now, I catch myself looking at my kids and trying and picture how it would feel to lose one of them. I know that sounds morbid, but I cannot help myself. When I am out walking with them and they are cycling or on their scooters, I have a premonition of one of them veering into the road or a car mounting the footpath. I feel physically sick thinking about it. I cannot imagine the pain Dad must have gone through, losing Tom. The feelings he must have had for the rest of his life.

It does not stop me from bringing them out on their bikes though. You cannot wrap them in cotton wool, cannot keep them safe from everything. I do not think Dad could have protected Tom from that crash. I do not blame him. It was an accident. The other driver was at fault. Tom was just unlucky. And I was just lucky.

What struck me about that time was I did not know what Dad did to pass the time when we were not there. He was alone in his house a lot. Sure, he had friends in the Golf Club, and he had his housekeeper come three times a week, and there were his group of local friends who he would meet sporadically. But he had no companionship. I still do not know if he ever considered dating again or even just looking for somebody to spend some time with. I should have talked to him about it more. I should have talked to him about it at all.

Maybe that what happens with relationships with your parents though? You take them for granted. You do not really ever consider what is going on in their lives, as long as everything is ok in yours. What I discovered when I became a father was that you never want to burden your children with your problems. You want them to be able to hang on to the naïve optimism that all children have. That everything is perfect. They do not care about what you do for a living or how much debt you may have. All they want is love and attention. And in return, they will give you theirs. Which is the best gift of all.

By the time Dad turned 80, it was clear he was going to need some help in the house. He had slowed down tremendously, and everything was becoming a bit of a struggle. Climbing the stairs was a worry and I was sure I would receive a phone call some night with him lying in a heap at the bottom of the staircase. I decided I needed to broach the subject of his moving out with him, so I went to see him on my own and asked him would he consider moving to Dublin. To an apartment near us. To my surprise, he agreed straight away. I guess he knew he could not be on his own much longer – and perhaps he was lonely. Once Dad made a decision on something, you had to move fast. If he was committed, you needed to get it done before he had a chance to change his mind.

Therefore, I searched online for a few suitable apartments and found one just around the corner from us – literally a 10-minute walk. Dad took one look and accepted. He decided to sell the house too. This was big moment for him. This was Mum and Dad's house. Where Tom and I had grown up. All those memories. Our home. I had always known that financially, in order for Dad to make the move to Dublin, he would need to sell, but seeing the For Sale sign outside our home and making the last trip to the house was an emotional day. We walked around the empty house, just the two of us, not talking to each other. Both deep in thought, lost in memories of our lives in the house. Memories of Tom and Mum. And memories of just the two of us, when the others had gone.

"Ah, well." Dad said with a tear in his eye. "Time for the next chapter, eh?"

It all happened so quickly. One month Dad was struggling around the old house and the next he was living around the corner in a new apartment. He was so close now that I saw him several times a week. He could walk to the shops, walk to the pub for a pint and to meet his friends. He was also close to his Grandkids who loved having him nearby. I would bring them to visit him every Saturday morning. Without fail. If we were late, Dad would ring to see where we were. I was a bystander. It was Becky and Matthew whom he wanted to see. He would sit beside them, giving out biscuits and asking questions about their week. He would draw pictures with them, colour with them. He simply had so much time for them. We would go for walks beside the river. Watching them grow up, from buggies, to scooters to bikes. He was such an active part in their lives.

Everything was working out perfectly. Dad was happy. I was happy. My family was beautiful and perfect. Life was great for 3 and a half years. We all made lots of new memories. He had Christmas Day in our house starting a new tradition.

Then, he began to get sick.

Chapter 17

Dublin, 2020.

I googled artists in Lithuania called Emilis and a few popped up on screen. One stood out, Emilis Petraitis, as the most popular. When I clicked through to images of his work, I could see I was on the right track as all the paintings were of the sea. The Baltic Sea. They were phenomenal – with some I had to double check I was not looking at an actual photographic image. They were also all very similar to the pieces I had on my desk. I scrolled through the images – then clicked back to see if I could find out some contact information. There was a website called Emilispetraitis.com – seemed like a good place to try. I clicked into it – and was greeted by a picture of a man far younger than I expected Emilis to be. I was trying to work out how old he must be now. If he was of similar age to Dad in 1991, or maybe even 10 years younger, he would be in mid to late 70's by now. However, this man looked in his late 40's, perhaps early 50's. Maybe this was not him. The page was in Lithuanian so I could not make any sense of it. I navigated through the website looking again at pages of incredibly lifelike sea images. I returned to the homepage, copied the text underneath the picture, and opened up the translator page I had used previously.

"Welcome to the website dedicated to the art and life of Emilis Petraitis. Emilis painted all the works of art you will see over the next few pages for himself. He never expected nor wanted his work to be made public. Emilis was a proud Lithuanian. In 1991, he disappeared on the night of Sausio įvykiai. *He was last seen approaching the tanks as they made their way towards the Vilnius TV Tower. His body was never recovered, and he has not been officially listed as one of the brave 14 heroes who lost their lives that night. His wife Lina and his daughter Audra were left with no answers and fleeing Vilnius in fear, they returned to Lina's home place in* Klaipėda. *There, the artwork was kept hidden from public view. It was cherished by Lina as her only link left to Emilis. She never gave up hope – all the while that no body was discovered, she held on to a shred of hope that Emilis was alive somewhere and would return to his family, just as he had done years before when he was banished to the notorious labour camp of Perm 36, one of the last labour camps to exist. However, he never returned. In 2001, Lina died not knowing what happened to her beloved Emilis. After her mother's death, Audra decided it was time to let the people of* Klaipėda *see her father's work. It was met with wild acclaim, first locally and then nationally. Soon, exhibitions were being set up all over Lithuania and the rest of the Baltic States. The Baltic Sea has long had an affection for these people and these paintings, as you will see, beautifully capture the beauty as well as the bleakness of 'Baltijos jura'. International*

acclaim also followed and Emilis is now recognised as one of the most prominent sea painters of his generation.

Audra has kept the spirit of her mother and father alive through his paintings. In her late brother's memory, she founded the Matis foundation – an artist programme providing scholarships for gifted painters and musicians from under privileged backgrounds at top colleges across the Baltic States and further afield. To date this foundation has helped over 30 talented students, several of whom have already broken through and ran exhibitions and concerts all throughout Europe. She continues to live in Klaipėda with her family, looking out to sea each day and thinking of her beloved Mother, Father and Brother."

I sat back and tried to take it all in. Emilis had not made it to Klaipėda at all. He was not safe. He had simply disappeared. No wonder nobody could contact him in the days and weeks after. Dad had been convinced from talking to the neighbour that they had all, Emilis, Lina and Audra, gone to Klaipėda – and he thought no more of it. He simply misunderstood what she said. She had meant that Lina and Audra had gone back to Klaipėda. His satisfaction that his friend was safe and was happy was shattered. I wonder did he ever try making contact again. Or did Mum's sickness and then looking after me simply get in the way. And what about the paintings I had in my hand – what were they worth and did Audra even know they existed?

I looked through the website looking for some contact details for Audra. There was just a generic information email address. I sent an email straight away.

"Dear Audra. My name is Will O'Connor, son of James O'Connor. My father had dealings with your father in 1991 in Vilnius and I wanted to check in with you to see if you remembered him. I would really like to catch up with you soon as I have something of your fathers I would like to return.

Thanks, Will."

I put my mobile phone number on the email too and pressed send. I spent another few minutes looking through the website. The paintings really were exceptional. He was an extremely talented artist and Audra had seemingly built up quite a business selling his work. As I was shutting down my laptop, my phone rang. It was a foreign number. I picked up at once.

"Will speaking."

"Hi, Will." It was a female's voice, heavily accented. "My name is Audra Petraitis.

My heart jumped. "Hi" I stuttered.

"I have just read your email. I am not usually in the office but happen to be here today. I remember your father. I remember he came to our apartment when I was a little girl. How are you"?

"I am great," I replied. "I can't believe you remembered him so quickly."

"Of course, I did. You said you have something of my fathers, but I also have something of your fathers."

I was not expecting that. A muttered "Oh" was all I could come up with.

"Your father gave Emilis his watch. My Mother kept hold of it for all those years and I wasn't sure why we had it, but assumed it had some significance, so I also have kept on to it."

"His watch," My mind went back to Dad lying in the hospital bed asking me about his second watch.

"What do you have of my father's?" she asked.

"Sorry, I should have told you first. I have some paintings – I have four paintings that your father gave to my dad. Three of which I had never seen before until last week."

This time it was Audra's turn to be shocked.

"That is amazing," she cried. "Obviously, we have no more original work from Emilis. I cannot believe there are new paintings out there. Are they of the sea?"

"Yes. They are beautiful. One has been hanging on my father's wall for the last 10 years. The others, I found stored in a cupboard when I was cleaning out my dad's apartment."

"Cleaning out his apartment. Is he okay?" she asked?

"No, unfortunately my father passed away a couple of weeks ago."

"Oh, no. I am so sorry to hear that. I often thought about your father when I would look at the watch. I should have reached out to try to make contact, but I had no idea where to start. I didn't even know what country he was from."

"We are in Ireland." I replied. "And I am so sorry about your father. And your mother. I was reading your story on the website – you have done an amazing job."

"Thank You – it is nice to keep a connection with Emilis and it helped me get over my Mum passing away. I would really like to see those paintings."

"Of course," I said. "I would also like to see the watch!"

We arranged a zoom call for the following day where we could both show off what we had.

"You know, Will, I remember your dad talking about you. He told me he had a son my age. I do not know why, but I always remembered that. I look forward to speaking to you tomorrow."

We signed off. I could not really believe what had just happened. In 5 minutes, I had discovered what the other watch was. I also started to think that these paintings might be also worth some serious money.

We spoke the next day on Zoom. Audra showed me the watch. She read out the engraving on the back. 'Tom. 25/08/76''. Tom's date of birth. I showed her the paintings. She was visibly emotional as she took them in, even across the internet. I asked her how she thought we might make an exchange.

"Will, these paintings are worth money. I cannot just exchange them. They are yours. My father gave them to your father. They are yours to sell. I simply wanted to see them and to arrange to give this watch back to you."

Audra told me that she was due in London in 2 weeks' time to open an exhibition of her father's work at an art college. It was also a chance for her to sell the scholarship programme.

"Perfect. I can come over to London to meet you and we can exchange them then."

"No exchange, Will!" she insisted.

"We will see," I laughed.

I travelled to London on my own. A day trip. I arrived in the city at 9:30 a.m. and went for a stroll, soaking in the hustle and bustle of the city. With COVID restrictions, it had been so long since I had been a tourist. I was meeting Audra at

10.30 at the Landmark Hotel in Marylebone. I arrived a little early and found a seat in the lobby. It was a magnificent hotel – a clear sign of how well she was doing for herself. I loved just sitting there, watching the comings and goings, trying to figure out where all these people were going or whom they were meeting. They possibly were doing the same about me.

I saw a tall, beautiful woman exit the lift in front of me. She was exquisitely dressed, designer sunglasses perched on her head. She was on the phone. I felt my own phone vibrate in my pocket. An unknown number. I answered.

"Will?" It was Audra.

"Hi, Audra. I am in the hotel lobby," I replied.

"Me too" I looked up and realized that the tall woman was talking to me on her phone. I hung up, stood up, and walked over to her.

"Audra?" She smiled.

"Will! How nice to meet you. Let's get some coffee."

We took a seat in the Garden Terrace and ordered.

"It's so good to meet you. Such a strange thing to get that email from you so out of the blue," Audra began.

"It's funny but I really do remember your father. He came to our apartment for a meal with my father. They seemed to be good friends. I remember practicing my English with him."

I smiled.

"It's strange, he never told me anything about Vilnius," I replied as the waiter delivered out coffees.

"Were you close to your father, Will?" she asked.

I pause and think about the question. I suppose I have a few answers I could give.

"I was in the last ten years. Before then we had a falling out for a while. Wasted some time."

"We cannot regret anything. Look at me. I only got to spend a short time with my father but I wouldn't change it for the world," she said with a smile.

"His paintings are incredible, Audra."

"I know. And he was so protective of them. He would not show them to anyone. I was surprised that your father got to see them! And to be given some – Emilis must have really liked him."

She went on to talk to me about her father. To tell his life story. She spoke with such affection about a man that she only managed to spend a mere seven short years with. He was obviously an extremely charismatic man. By the end of her tale, I wished I could have met him too. What also came across was the sorrow that she had suffered in her life. First her brother, then her father. Then her mother. Now she was the only one in her family left. It echoed my story. The details were different but the outcomes the same for both of us. I told her about Tom and my mother. I asked her about Matis. She spoke of how she lived with his ghost for all of her childhood.

"He was always there. The photographs were everywhere. My mother and father spoke of him all the time, I think to ensure they would not let his memory die. We celebrated his birthday every year. I began to resent him terribly. He was stealing my life. I was reminded numerous times that he died on his way to get a present for me. As if, it was somehow my fault. I do not think my father ever recovered from hearing the news about Matis. It was the thoughts of Matis and my mother that got him through his time in the labour camp. To come home and have this taken away was heartbreaking, even if he did get to meet me for the first time."

"How old were you when your father disappeared?" I asked.

"I had just turned 11. The tenth anniversary of Matis's death. Even my birthday will always be linked to him. It was the night after you father was at our apartment. He left to go for a meal with his friends. And we never saw him again."

"My father was at that meal with Emilis," I said watching the shock on Audra's face. I proceeded to tell her the story that Ben had told me about that night in Vilnius.

As I finished, I could see tears in her eyes.

"I wish I could have met your father, Will. Maybe he knew something that could help explain what happened. Someone he saw or something Emilis said to him."

"And Emilis was never seen again," I asked.

"No. We tried everything. Nobody had a lead. It was as if he vanished into thin air. For years, my mother thought he had escaped somewhere. That he would return as he had before. Arrive on our doorstep in Klaipėda unexpectedly. However, it never happened. I think she still thought it might happen, right up to her dying day."

"We found out that he was a member of the Sąjūdis," she stopped, as I look confused.

"They were the Reform Movement of Lithuania. They were formed to seek independence for Lithuania. They helped organise The Baltic Way." I nodded. I had heard of that alright.

"We never knew he was a member. My mother remembers him telling her that he thought Jurgis, his best friend from growing up together, was a member. Turns out it was him all the time. It explains why he was there that night. It might explain why he disappeared."

"For years, I hated him. I hated that he had left us again. That he had left me. But then I began to look at his paintings again and I could take some joy from them. It seemed like the obvious thing to do was for us to sell them. My Mother and I were not rich; my mother worked three jobs when I was in school. But she would not hear of it. She would tell me he didn't want them made public."

"When she died, I wrestled with myself as to what to do. I showed an artist friend of mine. He convinced me what I already knew – that they were beautiful, and people needed to see them. So, I did. And here we are. I thought I had seen them all until you emailed me."

We had been sitting talking for nearly 2 hours. The waiter was hovering around our table.

"Let's get some lunch," I suggested. Audra agreed so we took a break from our reminiscing, ordered, and ate some lunch. We talked about our lives now. She was separated. Her marriage only lasted 5 years but she had two beautiful children. A boy and a girl. Like me. We swapped pictures.

"Tell me about the foundation?" I asked as we ordered more coffee.

Her eyes lit up as she described what she had set up.

"It has helped me make peace with both Matis and Emilis. Matis did not deserve my resentment. He was just a boy. He did nothing wrong. I am so sad I did not get to meet him properly, to spend my life with him. I named the foundation in his honour because I wanted to celebrate his life. We have helped so many young people – young Balkans. The people who my father would have wanted to help. He loved his country. He desperately wanted Lithuania to be truly free. He would be so proud to see us as a country now, in the world on our own two feet."

"Now, Will, you have kept me waiting long enough. Let me see those paintings!" She laughed.

I took out the canvases and showed them to her. She smiled and nodded at each of them in turn.

"Yes. They are originals, alright!"

It had not crossed my mind that she thought I might be a fraud with some fakes. I laughed.

"I will sell these for you very easily, I could probably find a buyer here in London," she said taking out her phone. "Let me make a quick call."

"I don't want to sell the paintings, Audra."

"They are yours. I did not even know they existed until a couple of weeks ago. And if my father had wanted to sell them, he would have done so years ago. He sat in the same chair every day in his apartment you know. And this picture, I show her the one I had removed from the frame before I left home; this one was always behind him. I never properly asked him about it. I have a vague recollection of him telling me it was of the Baltic Sea, but nothing more about it or where he got it. I took his chair from his apartment. It is in my living room now. And this painting sat behind it. Keeping guard."

She smiles at me; I can see the relief in her eyes, but she clearly does not know how to progress. I make a suggestion.

"These should stay in Lithuania. I do not think you should sell them at all. Looking at where we are sitting and all this luxury, I am guessing you do not need the money. I think both our fathers would like that. Perhaps you could donate them to the National Museum of Art. That way they can always be appreciated by Lithuanians."

Audra smiled broadly, "I love that idea! Thank you, Will."

She suddenly turns to me, "I nearly forgot. Here," and she thrust a box to me. I open it – it is my father's watch. When I see it in my hands, I suddenly remember it vividly on his wrist as I was growing up. When I was much younger. I turn it over in my hand and look at the engraving on the back. I smile but inside I have differing emotions. I think of Tom. I think of Dad wearing this watch after he died. I wonder why Dad did not have watch with my name engraved when I was born. The old feelings of resentment towards my brother return from nowhere.

I catch myself.

"Thank you," I say to Audra.

We sit talking for a while longer until I realise, I will have to go in order to make my flight.

"Thank you so much for reaching out, Will. I am so happy to have these back."

She paused and handed me back the picture I removed from the frame.

"I think you should keep this one. Put it back over your father's chair. Let it watch over you."

I smiled and thanked her.

We hug and I am walking away when she turns and calls me back.

"Treasure all the time you spent with you father and Brother, Will. Do not waste time thinking of the bad times. Life is too short."

With that, she turns and is gone. I stand in the lobby for a moment, considering her words.

She is right. Life is too short.

I think back to a time Dad and I met for a pint. It was August 25, 2016. Tom's 40th Birthday. I had not understood the significance of the date when he suggested we go for a pint. Before we drank our first sip, Dad raised a glass – 'to Tom on his 40th. To the man he would have become. To both of us missing having a pint with him.' I touched my glass against his.

"I can't believe he would have been 40 today," Dad said.

"Christ, Will, I miss him every day. I know, I know I'm not meant to say that in front of you, but I do."

"Dad," I start, "Jesus! Of course, I know you miss him. I miss him too."

"I can remember the day he was born." Dad continues. "I was at home. Back then, the husband did not really go to the hospital. There was a couple of lads putting a roof on our garage. I got the call from your mum's sister to tell me it was a boy. I was so happy. I called the two lads in, and we had a drink of whiskey at the kitchen table."

I smile to myself. My favourite story about me being born, eh?

Dad looks at me.

"Will. It is not a competition you know. I loved the two of you the same. We will never know what our lives could have been like. With Tom. Then with Mum. We should be all sitting here now, all getting old together. Having a big party for Toms 40th. As a family, I have never felt as alone as when you were in Australia. I knew you had to go. I knew it was good for you, good for us. Nevertheless, I missed you every day and I wanted you to come home every day. I see you now. Your life. Your beautiful wife and beautiful children. My little Becky. My star. And Matthew. My Matthew. He is going to be a topper. You have it all, Will. You are so lucky. And I am so lucky to be a part of it. I am so proud of you." Dad was choking back on tears.

"We can't look back in regret all our lives. We have to live. To move on. I will be gone soon too. Then it will be just you left from our family. I was like you are now. My life with my young family stretched out ahead of me. Treasure it, Will. Treasure it all." He took a gulp from his pint and looked away into the distance.

I had no response. I drank my pint. It was all I could do to not break down in tears sitting at the bar.

On my trip home on the flight from London, I think of all the good times I shared with each of them, either all together or individually. Dad, Tom and Mum. My family. My lovely family. I am smiling as the plane lands back in Dublin.

Chapter 18

Klaipėda, 1998.

James was early for the meeting. As usual. 30 minutes early. He sat at the café, nursing his coffee, looking out at the magnificent Baltic Sea. It was calm today. It was late summer and there were many people around enjoying the beautiful weather. He began to feel nervous. He was not sure what to expect from the meeting. It had been over 7 years.

He had arrived in Vilnius 2 days previously. He met with Jurgis, and they had a lovely meal, reminiscing about the old days. Jurgis had a new restaurant. He had sold his old place. He was badly injured on the night of Bloody Sunday. James was keen to find out what happened, not only to Jurgis but also to Emilis.

"It is the strangest thing James" Jurgis started.

"One minute he was standing beside me. We were all shouting at the tanks as they made their way towards us. Then the gunfire started, and everybody started to run. There was such panic, such confusion. But Emilis was definitely beside me. The next minute I looked, and he was gone. Simply disappeared. I turned to look for him but as I did, I was pushed over by others looking to run away. I fell awkwardly and ended up breaking my hip. It was agony. I could not move.

The pain was nearly unbearable. I ended up lying there for two hours before an ambulance came to me. I saw them all die. I saw the Soviets firing at them. I saw them fall. I was terrified. Terrified that they would shoot me where I lay. But they did not. They left me. I think I passed out for a while. Then the ambulances arrived, and I was taken away. I ended up having to spend 6 weeks in hospital. I got in contact with everybody I knew in Vilnius and beyond, to see where Emilis had ended up. Nobody had seen or heard from him. It was as if he simply vanished into thin air."

Jurgis told James how his network had searched and searched for Emilis in the weeks and months that followed. However, there was no sign of him. Lina and Audra had decided to go back to Klaipėda. Jurgis left hospital and sold his restaurant. He needed more time to recuperate. Lithuania was free. It was the moment that he had been waiting for all his life, but he felt he could not enjoy it properly without his best friend by his side.

"What do you think happened to him?" asked James.

"I truly do not know. I have a couple of theories. The first one is that he ran. He saw trouble and thought he was in danger, so he ran. He somehow got out of the country. He could not have known that we would be free so soon after. And wherever he went to, something happened to him, perhaps he had an accident, and he died. He would not have stayed away. He could not have stayed away from his beloved Lina and Audra." Jurgis paused to compose himself.

"The second theory, and the one I believe more, is that he was killed that night. Either shot there at the TV tower or taken away and shot later. They took his body and dumped it somewhere. Somewhere it would not be found. Emilis was part of the Sąjūdis, you know. They would have known his name, known his face. You saw him that night James. He was standing up tall, prepared to take those tanks on for his country. Therefore, I think someone on their side identified him and they made decision to take him out. And they did. There will be no fairy-tale ending. He will not return as he did before. We will not see that big smile and loud laugh and we will not get to celebrate our country together. And more than that and perhaps worse than that, his name is not associated with Sausio įvykiai There is no memorial for Emilis. He will not have a street named after him. He is officially missing. He is not a hero to Lithuania. People here do not know his story, even though I try to tell it as much as I can."

Jurgis sits back and closes his eyes. James is transported back to that night. Back to realising how close he was to real danger. How stupid he was to risk his life by running through the streets with Emilis, caught up in the excitement. How lucky he was that Ben and Alex arrived when they did.

They finish their meal and James asks Jurgis if he could organise a meeting in Klaipėda for him. Jurgis promises to do his best and will contact James at the hotel.

And so now, James is sitting at the café waiting. He sees her through the window. She looks older, but still just as beautiful. Lina. She enters the cafe and James jumps to his feet. He is not sure if she will recognise him or even remember him at all. From what he could remember, her English was not great either. She smiles as she sees him stand and makes her way over to him.

"James! How nice to see you," she gives him a kiss.

"Lina. I was not sure if you would remember me."

179

"Of course, I do. I remember you and Emilis being drunk as fools and waking up the entire apartment block in the middle of the night!" She laughed, "Anyway, I've been carrying this around with me for 7 years so how could I forget you?"

She places a watch on the table. James's watch.

James looks at it. "That's not why I came, Lina," he said suddenly worried that she thought he has travelled here just to get his watch back.

"Why are you here then, James?" she asked, ordering a coffee off a passing waiter.

"I wanted to see how you are. I wanted to find out about Emilis." He replied.

"I was there that night, Lina. I saw him as I left. He was very much alive. I just wanted to know what happened to my friend. And to make sure you and Audra were ok. Up until a couple of months ago, I thought Emilis, you and Audra were all living here safely."

Lina sat back in her chair. James realised it was not necessarily older that she looked. She looked sad. And weary.

"I do not know what happened to Emilis" she began. "He simply never came home that night. I knew what was happening. All of Vilnius knew what was happening. And I knew my Emilis would be stuck in the middle of it. He could not help himself. He promised me so many times that would not get into any more trouble, that he would not leave us again. But here we are." She looked out the window to the sea, tears in her eyes.

"I was frantic for those couple of days. Nobody seemed to know a thing. There had been deaths but when the names were published of the 13 that died, Emilis was not one of them.

180

Jurgis was in hospital so he could not help me. I suddenly became very scared. I decided to take Audra and come back here to Klaipėda, where I am from. I knew Emilis would know where we went. And I waited. Days turned into weeks and into months. No word. He had vanished. I felt like the whole of Vilnius was looking for him. But nothing. I had to get on with my life. Audra needed me. And so, I did. That is now 7 years ago. And I still do not know what happened to him."

They sat in silence for a couple of minutes, both looking out at the Baltic Sea. Then James told Lina about his life. He told her about Tom. He told her about Will. And he told her about Maria. His beautiful Maria. When he was finished, he smiled at Lina.

"Our stories are similar, Lina. We have both loved and lost."

"They are," she agreed. "Sometimes I think Emilis will appear at my door again. Like he did all those years ago. I feel like I have lost him twice. However, I know that will not happen. Although they will not announce it officially, I know my Emilis is dead."

"But we are lucky, James. We are lucky that we had these people in our lives. Matis, Emilis, Tom and Maria. And now we still have Audra and Will." She continued.

"Audra is everything to me now. I do not know what I would do without her. It must be the same with you and Will. We cannot let their lives be defined by the death of others a long time ago. It is not their fault. They are victims of circumstance. They did not ask to be born into all this death, grief, and sorrow. Audra makes me get up every morning. She is my reason for being. I see both Matis and Emilis in her. The way she talks, the way she walks, the time she spends with people. And she is my connection to them too. Especially Emilis. I feel closer to him when I am with Audra. But I do not know why I am telling you all this, you must feel the same way with Will."

James paused. Did he? He felt that he had been holding in his grief because of Will. Especially the grief over Tom. And he resented Will for that. He felt he could not talk about Tom as much as he would like to for fear of hurting Will's feelings. It was one of the reasons why he was ok with the fact he had given away his watch – he did not want Will to be reminded of the fact that he wore a watch with Tom's name on it. And that was not fair on himself. Or Will for that matter. As Lina said, he did not do anything to deserve this. He vowed not to make the same mistake with Maria's death. He would talk to Will about it. Open up to him. They would need to get through this together. To live their lives.

James opened his bag and took out the paintings Emilis had given him. He passed them over to Lina. "These are yours," he said.

She looked at them on the table. She shook her head.

"I do not want these, James. Emilis gave them to you. Anyway, I have hundreds of them taking up space at home."

"Would you not show them to somebody, Lina, they are really good?"

"I know they are. But you heard what he was like. These were his. He did not want anyone to see them. I cannot go against his wishes now. No, I will just keep them. I will leave them for Audra. She can decide what to do with them when I am gone."

James smiled. He took the paintings back and passed the watch back over.

"Very well. Then keep this too. I will leave the paintings for Will. Audra and Will can decide what to do with them all."

Lina laughed. "Really James. You do not want your watch back?" she asked.

"I have survived without it. I have a new one now." He laughed pointing at his wrist.

They sat in the café for another hour, chatting, getting to know each other. Two people, linked by circumstance. James commented on her English. Lina told him Audra had taken her on as a pupil and taught her every day.

"She is a very strict teacher." She laughed. When it was time to leave, James gave Lina his phone number.

"Keep in touch Lina. If you ever need anything or if I can help with anything, let me know," he said.

"Thanks, James. Good luck with your life. Try to live. And let Will live his life."

James left and walked out into the sunshine. He stood and looked out at the Baltic Sea. It really was beautiful. He remained there for a while, thinking about Emilis, Lina, and Audra. About their loss. And about how strong Lina was. He thought about Tom. And how he missed him every day. And he thought about Maria. Only gone a couple of years but already such a void in his life. Finally, he thought about Will. He needed to get home to Will. They needed to begin their new lives together.

Chapter 19

Dublin, January 2020.

I sit in my chair, looking out at the river. It is the same scene I see every day, but it is always changing. Changing with the seasons, changing with the people who walk by and the wildlife I see. I have lived here for nearly 4 years now. I like it. I am close to Will and his family. I am close to my friends. I knew I had to leave my house. In the end, Will thought it was his idea for me to leave. But I had already made up my mind. A couple of falls down the stairs had made the decision easy for me. I never told Will I fell; I know he would have overreacted. It was difficult leaving. So many memories in that house. Memories of my family. I can remember moving in there with Maria. We were just married. Everything was ahead of us. Plans for a family. Plans for our life together. Tom and Will arrived, and we were so happy. I travelled a lot with work but that was how we managed to afford to live in the house. Maria was an amazing Mother to those boys. They adored her. I was secondary, I knew that. However, I loved them too. I loved playing with them in our garden. Long football matches with no winner. When Tom died, Maria and I talked about selling up and moving house. To get away from the memories. But in the end, we decided to stay. To feel *closer to Tom. When I was on my own in the house, when Will had gone to Australia, those same memories terrified me. I would be upstairs, and I could swear I could hear Tom and Maria downstairs. Every bit of the house reminded me of them. In the end, I was happy to leave.*

Maria and I had such plans for our old age. We would be together, just the two of us again, and we would travel. I would show her the world that I had been lucky enough to see throughout my life. We would grow old together, looking after each other. We had bets on who would go first. We both always assumed it would be me. I still cannot believe that she is gone. That she left me. In a couple of days, it will be 24 years. 24 years without her. She was only 51 years of age. Far too young. I did not think I would survive without her. Losing Tom was awful, but we had each other. And we had Will. Now I was on my own. Will was nearly grown up and in boarding school. He did not need the burden of looking after his old man weighing him down.

I had a bad relationship with my father. He barely talked to me but hit me regularly. I was an annoyance to him. My brother Joe was his favourite. I faded into the background. It ruined my relationship with my mother too. I could not understand how she could stand by and watch. I could not wait to leave home and did so the first chance I got at 18. I did not see my father again after that; he died when I was 20. My Mother died when I was 25. We had developed a better relationship for the last couple of years of her life. I always promised myself that I would have a different relationship with my children, if I was ever lucky enough to have any. I promised myself I would never, ever hit them. I nearly managed it. I think I had a strong connection to my boys. I think they loved me. I certainly loved them. I never hit Tom. Perhaps I never got the chance. I regret hitting Will every day since it happened. It came from nowhere. I was disgusted with myself afterwards. He left the house. And I did not see him for 7 years. Seven whole years. And I could not complain. I missed him terribly. I would write to him when he was in Australia. Silly letters, just to keep in touch. All I wanted to do was ask him to come back. However, I could not. He needed his space. I had let him down. My relationship with Will changed in that instant.

I replay the crash most days too. The light was orange. I know it was. But still. I could have slowed down. I could have stopped at the lights and waited. What would have happened to all of our lives if I had? How would Tom have turned out? Would I have ended up hitting him too I wonder? Would we all be together now? Or would I still be sitting here on my own, looking out at the river.

Sport was always our thing, Will and I. We were both never very good at articulating how we felt, but not when it came to sport. Any sport. But particularly Manchester United, specifically Roy Keane and Eric Cantona. And Golf. Shane Lowry. Sitting in Will's house last year watching Shane win The Open was one my greatest highlights. Because I got to watch it with Will. When he was in Australia, every time a match was on, rugby, soccer, hurling, anything, I would miss him. I picked up the phone so many times to call him. But put it down again. Lost my nerve. So, I would write another letter.

He lives around the corner. He has a beautiful family. His wife, Charlotte, is a topper. And his children! Becky is 100 miles an hour. She is a tornado. I love it. Nothing is too much for her. She is nonstop and into everything. And Matthew.

Matthew is a wonderful boy. Quiet but assured. He lets his sister take the limelight. However, a smile from Matthew is worth the world. He reminds me so much of Will. That quiet confidence. At least, he reminds me of Will before Tom died. I wish I could live long enough to see them both grow up. To see how Becky will turn out. I hope she remains true to herself. And to see what becomes of Matthew.

I fear I will not though. I am getting slower. And I am tired. All the time. I am pretty sure there is something wrong. I have been to the doctor, but he has not found anything of note. Yet. "Just old age I'm afraid James," he tells me. But I think it is more than that.

Every night I wake several times – the joy of old age – to go to the bathroom. The same predicament also has me awake before the dawn. In that half-light, lying in my bed, for a fleeting moment before I am fully awake and realise where I am, I think I am back in my home. Maria is beside me in the bed and Tom and Will are safe in their rooms. I am happy. Then I wake fully and reality hits. I am here, alone.

I think I am approaching the end. I have had a good life I suppose. I have seen a lot, travelled a lot. I was lucky enough to meet Maria and spend 26 unforgettable years with her. I had my two boys. There has been grief, sorrow and sadness. But overall, I am happy. The last 5 years have been amongst the happiest of my life, even without my Maria. I sometimes wonder should I have tried to find somebody new. For companionship. But I am glad I did not. I prefer to be here. Alone. But never lonely. I am filled with my thoughts and memories.

I think about Emilis most days. I wonder what happened to him. I only knew him for a couple of days, but he struck such a chord with me. I think I knew something was wrong when I travelled back to Vilnius in 1991. I had a sense he had not simply moved to Klaipėda. But I wanted everything to be ok for him. When I returned home, Maria became sick, so Emilis moved to the back of my mind. I kept in contact with Lina after I visited her in Klaipėda. We would talk on the phone every month. Just a quick check in. I could sense her getting weaker. Becoming more and more tired. She died in 2001. Broken hearted. I decided not to attend the funeral. I did not contact Audra. I felt it was time to leave her to her life. I read an article with interest last year outlining the success she has made from her father's paintings. It is remarkable. I think the time might now be right for me to give her back the paintings that I have. I framed one of them, my favourite one, and I keep it above my chair. I would not like to give that one back. Perhaps Will and I could travel to meet her. A trip. Just the two of us. I could get my watch back. I should suggest it soon. Or else it might be too late for me.

The sun is going down now on another day. I feel tired. Dreadfully tired. I wonder what I will eat tonight. I have no energy to cook. Perhaps I will skip dinner. Will and the kids will be in to see me in the morning. My favourite time of the week. They can pick me up something nice in the shop. I think I will just go to bed and sleep. I hope I dream of Maria and Tom.

Chapter 20

At the very start of Covid 19, I took dad for a walk with the kids to a park beside where we live. There is a large lake there and we sat for a while watching two adult swans caring for their five newly born cygnets. Becky and Matthew marvelled at the baby swans and Dad explained to them how they would grow up right there on the lake until they became big enough to fly away and start lives of their own. It is not a long walk to Dad's apartment, but it took us hours to get home. I suddenly realised how weak and frail he had become. He was gripping onto my arm shuffling slowly all the way but still fully involved in the conversation with my children talking to them and giving both of them his undivided attention.

We went back to the lake last week. Just me, Becky and Matthew. It is November now; the leaves have gone and the air is cold. The two swans are alone on the lake; their cygnets have grown up and left. The end of another chapter. Becky, my daughter, puts her hand in mine and looked up at me.

"They have left us, just like Grandpa." She smiled sadly.

Sitting here now, I wonder how Dad would feel how this has all panned out. I am not overly religious – but I feel his presence near me. He must have known that someday, somebody would have found the paintings. Perhaps he wanted it to be me. Perhaps he was still planning to try to contact Emilis one day. Maybe he did not know it was coming towards the end at all.

I take a trip to his grave with my family. Mum and Tom are buried there too. I like to think of them together. For all time. It is a beautiful place surrounded by farmland and it is busy. Several families are there, and a farmer is tending to his fields that border the graveyard on all sides. My son Matthew and I leave the girls at the car and approach the grave. Kneeling, I take the watch out of my pocket and dig a small hole near the headstone. The watch is wrapped in a cloth, and I place it in the hole, covering it back in. It is back with him now. He is the rightful owner, not me.

"I got your watch back, Dad. You were right about the two watches. I'm sorry I doubted you and thought you had gone mad!"

I close my eyes feeling the winter sun on my face. I can see him. He is standing in Cathedral Square in Vilnius, facing away from me. He looks younger than I remember. Possibly in his late 40's or early 50's. He has more hair and he is tanned and slim. The sun is shining and there are people everywhere. They are waving flags and it looks like a celebration of some sort. Dad is holding the hand of a young boy – I cannot see his face, but I can tell from the back of his head that it is Tom. I call his name, but he does not hear me. Out of the corner of my eye, I see a large man ambling towards him. There is a boy perched on his shoulders. He is calling out to Dad. Dad turns and a huge smile breaks out on his face. They embrace, standing on the bridge. They look like two old friends reunited. It is Emilis. They begin to move away, and I try to call out again. Suddenly Dad seems to hear me. He turns around to face me. My dad. He waves and blows a kiss. I see his watch is on his wrist. "Thank you," he mouths.

"I love you," I shouted back. "I miss you."

He smiles broadly at me, waves again, turns back to Emilis and they set off away from me. I watch them go, moving into the crowds of people until I can no longer see them.

I open my eyes and I am back at the grave.

My son is tugging at my arm, "Dad, are you okay?"

"Yes," I reply. "I am great. Let's go, will we?"

We walk off holding hands and head back to the car. I turn and take one last look back at my father's grave and smile. I am happy he is at peace. In the distance I can see Charlotte and Becky at the car, laughing.

I turn to my son, "I love you."

"I love you more, Dad," he replied smiling up at me.

"Impossible, Matthew. Impossible."

THE END